BUSINESS & PLEASURE

CASTILLE HOTEL SERIES-BOOK 1

ALEXIS WINTER

A NOVEL

BY

Alexis Winter

RICH. ARROGANT. SO DROP DEAD
SEXY YOU'RE READY TO SELL YOUR
KIDNEY JUST TO TOUCH HIM.

Did I mention he's technically my new boss?

You know the type…

Every man wants to be him and every woman wants him.

Mr. Never-Goes-Home-With-The-Same-Woman- Twice guy.

I hate him but also…

Why can't I stop myself from seeing him on top of me every time I
close my eyes?

Yeah…I'm screwed.

All I have to do is follow the rules.
1. Don't sleep with the sexy, arrogant prick.
2. Don't drool every time you look at his perfectly chiseled face and
rock-hard body.
3. But mostly…don't let him know you want him just as bad.

Then again…rules are meant to be broken.

Can a no-strings-attached fling blossom into actual, head-over-heels love or will I ruin my career when I finally slap that smug grin off his panty-melting face?

❀ Created with Vellum

ALLISON

Life has a funny way of not turning out the way you thought it would. Sometimes it's irony, other times it's a full-blown quarter-life crisis staring you in the face at twenty-five years old...in an airport bathroom.

It's crazy how one minute, you have your entire life planned out, and in a few short hours and a few impulsive, if not reckless, decisions later, your life has jumped the tracks and is now aimlessly barreling ahead at full speed.

I splash cold water on my face and take in a few deep breaths, hoping it will calm the symphony of butterflies in my stomach. My knuckles have gone white as I grip the edge of the sink, willing myself to stay calm and pull it together. I hardly notice the endless stream of fellow travelers coming in and out.

Once I'm calm enough, I reach into my purse and pull out a few makeup items to freshen myself up. What's that stupid quote about giving a woman the right lipstick and she can conquer the world? Yeah, okay, show me that color, please. The woman who penned that never had a quarter-life crisis in a public restroom.

After a little self-care and a mental pep talk, I feel good enough to emerge from my hideout, if only to make a beeline for the nearest bar.

I feel a buzzing in my pocket as I exit the restroom and pull out my phone to check my messages.

"Uggghhh, goddammit!" I groan petulantly as I read the 'your flight is now delayed' text from my airline. I even throw in a foot stomp for emphasis as I roll my eyes and grab my bag, heading off in search of that bar.

Locating a decent-looking watering hole, I pull up my bag to a barstool and dramatically flop onto the seat. The bartender gives me a nod as if to say he sees me and will be over in a moment. I don't even need to look at the menu to know what I want.

I wasn't a big drinker in college, despite a stressful double major and a demanding internship. I enjoy a nice glass of wine now and then, but when I need to calm my nerves or feel a buzz, I always go for a dirty vodka martini with extra olives. I rattle off my order to the bartender when he finally saunters over, barely giving him the chance to get out his pleasantries.

The bar is dimly lit, even for an airport. It's located in a more obscure part of the terminal and seems to be the bar people go to when they have a long layover or are stuck with a shitty delay like myself. I barely have the first sip of my very overpriced martini when I feel the familiar presence of a once-popular frat boy lingering near me. Why do they all feel the need to douse themselves in enough mediocre cologne to offend anyone within a fifty-yard radius?

I set my drink back down when he leans himself against the bar, half-pressing himself against my arm as if personal space is a thing of the past.

"Looks like you could use another," he says as he sloppily points to my very full martini glass.

"I haven't even had a full drink of this one yet but thank you." I smile politely but turn away quickly so as not to encourage him. This isn't my first rodeo; I am very aware of the effect I have on men. I was blessed by the genetic gods with piercing blue eyes and naturally thick blonde hair. I'm not Barbie height, merely five-six, but I don't have to do much to keep my hourglass figure and perky C-cups. I can't complain, and I certainly don't take it for granted, but it pretty much

2

attracts douchebags like it's their job. Sometimes I feel bad for them that they can't seem to resist a full-breasted blonde woman. Very predictable, and very pathetic.

My friends had given me the nickname Barbie since I was about thirteen years old. At the time, I had outgrown pretty much everyone in my grade and was the only middle schooler that stood head and shoulders above everyone else and had a full chest. Unfortunately, I stopped growing that same year. When I was younger, I was mortified by the attention my body got me; it was awkward as hell to be the only fifth grader wearing a sport's bra at recess to play kickball.

"So where you headed to? You live here in Dallas? I'd love to take you out sometime if you do. Or, hey, even if you don't, I'd fly to take you out!" He gestures wildly as he speaks, almost too confident that his offer to take me out will surely melt my panties and leave me begging him for happily ever after.

"No, no, I'm not local, and you haven't even asked my name or introduced yourself, but you want to take me out?" He quickly jumps in and cuts me off, thrusting his hand out to grasp mine.

"Trevor—"

I hold up my hand to stop him as I interject, "Don't bother. I won't remember it, and I won't be accepting the offer to hang out. I have had one helluva day, so if you don't mind, I'm going to drink this overpriced and watered-down martini in relative peace, ok?" I smile to soften the blow, but it doesn't seem to help.

He rolls his eyes and backs away with his hands in the air as if to say he surrenders. Something tells me he's probably been in trouble for his behavior in the past.

"You know, you blonde bitches are all the same. Your loss, sweetheart," he slurs. I lift my martini glass to him with a huge grin as I turn back around to face the bar and drown my sorrows.

Relieved to no longer be gagging on the syrupy-sweetness of his cologne, I drum my fingers on the bar, unsure of what to do with myself or my time. Normally, I would be elbows deep in a design, but since I had unceremoniously walked in on my ex banging someone else, I wasn't exactly in the headspace.

"That was a pretty brutal rejection; you seem well practiced at it though."

I haven't even noticed the man sitting to my left. There is an empty stool between us, but he clearly overhead my conversation with cologne boy. I turn my head to give him a snarky remark, but my words catch in my throat and I quickly down two large gulps of my martini. The liquor burns my throat, but it allows me the few extra seconds I need to gather my thoughts.

This guy looks like he walked out of a catalog called *Sexiest Men Alive*. I know that's a stupid way to describe someone but imagine all those guys that are in luxury car commercials and Ralph Lauren ads. The ones that somehow look like they work on Wall Street, are a secret agent, and could also be the leader of the free world while saving babies in their spare time...that's this guy. It looks like the Greek gods hand-carved this guy to be their fucking mascot.

He cradles a tumbler of amber liquid as he shoots me a coy smile, waiting for my response. His hair looks like waves of dark chocolate with a dusting of gray at the temples, and his eyes are the most vibrant green I have ever seen. The way his tailored suit hugs his body, I can imagine he keeps himself in amazing shape. Realizing I'm staring uncomfortably long at this stranger, I smile and shrug my shoulders at him, clearly still at a loss for forming coherent thoughts like a functioning adult.

"Cheers to a shitty day. I heard you tell Trevor over there that you had a helluva day and I can commiserate with you there."

"Who?" I can feel my face wrinkle in confusion.

"The lovely gentleman that just approached you," he says, gesturing with a nod towards the table of rowdy frat guys.

"Oh! Sorry, I guess I didn't even catch his name." I shrug my shoulders again as if this is the only form of primitive communication I'm capable of. I usually wasn't so callous, but like I told Trevor, today is not my day.

He lifts his almost empty glass in the air towards me and then swallows down the rest of the liquor. Almost without hesitation, the bartender scurries over and offers him another drink in a fresh glass.

4

I raise my martini back to him and take another long sip. "The fucking worst," I mutter almost to myself.

"Swap stories? Wallow without judgment?" he asks with a raised eyebrow and a sexy smirk.

I look down at my phone to check the time. "Might as well since my flight has been delayed for three hours."

He slides off his stool and settles back onto the one closest to me. He leans in, holding out his hand to me. I reach my hand out to meet him, very aware of my grossly sweaty palms. Of course, he smells fantastic. Like a fucking fantasy: expensive and refined with notes of sandalwood and oud.

"Vincent Crawford." He shakes my hand firmly as he raises an eyebrow as if to ask my name in return. A current of electricity travels through my body at his touch. Yup, this is the kind of guy who could completely fuck up your life in two-point-five seconds.

"Alison. Alison Ryder," I say, trying not to stare at his full lips.

"Well, since I offered, I'll go first, then you can decide how much you want to share to make me feel better about whining to a stranger." I laugh a little as he moves the glass back and forth between his hands.

"So, I work for a luxury hotel chain based in Chicago. I am currently in the middle of an acquisition in London and another possible one in Toronto. I am actually on my way to Canada now to meet with the current owner of a hotel there, after which I go home for a week or so, then off to London."

I sip my martini as he continues to expound on his travel plans that will be taking place over the next several months and the time it took to get everything organized.

"So anyway, my executive assistant that helped me plan all of these trips was supposed to travel with me, but today, she up and quit because she fell in love and eloped. This caused a chain reaction of events: since she quit, she didn't confirm my travel plans with my private jet, so they ended up submitting flight plans too late to get approved. Now I'm stuck on a commercial flight, which is getting me into Toronto at an ungodly hour, if it departs in the next hour as scheduled and causing me to miss my initial meeting."

I can see he is getting more and more exasperated, although he's barely changed his cadence or demeanor, remaining calm. He's clearly a meticulous and punctual man who doesn't appreciate being late or having his schedule interrupted.

"Jesus, that sounds like a nightmare. I'm sorry. Is your boss at least being understanding about everything?"

He stares into his glass as he swirls the remaining liquor around before downing it. He shakes his head as he swallows. "Sorry, I forgot to mention, I am the boss. I own the company, so it's just frustrating me more than normal that I am now stuck with no assistant to help me as I manage this possible new acquisition. Normally I'm very easy going, I like to think of myself as laid back, but when it comes to the reputation of my company, I can't help but get a little riled up."

"Hey, I get it. I'm very type-A, so I can imagine how frustrating that would be. When's your next trip after this one? Do you have time to hire an executive assistant before then?"

"I'll be in Toronto for four days, so I'll have about ten days to interview and hire a new EA before flying to London for other business. I sent an email to my vice president's secretary to see if she can help me get the ball rolling. The hard part will be finding someone willing to travel all over the damn globe almost immediately after starting. I prefer to build trust with someone before exposing them to such confidential information and putting those kinds of demands on them. Anyway, at this point, I'm just complaining. Your turn," he says, raising his empty glass to me.

"Well, we did agree we would wallow without judgment." I finish the rest of my martini before launching into my story.

"Funny enough, I am also from Chicago. Well—originally I'm from North Dakota, but I moved to Chicago for college and stayed because, well, it's Chicago!" I'm rambling like a ditzy high schooler, my hands gesturing a bit wildly. I don't know if it's the alcohol, the frazzled state of my nerves, or the sexy stranger that has me acting completely out of character.

"I'm an associate at a very prestigious design firm, Madeline Dwyer Designs...I did my internship there through undergrad and then worked my way up from junior associate to associate...working towards senior and then partner, or maybe owning my own firm someday. My fiancé is a senior associate at a big law firm, about to be made partner. He and I have been together for six years. I met him when I was still in school. I was working through my internship and went to a local bar where the lawyers from his firm frequented. He was a junior associate at the time." I let out a big breath to gather my thoughts and try to slow the two martinis from going straight to my head.

"So anyway, he proposed seven months ago, and we set a date for June of next year. Recently, his firm's Dallas office took on a huge class-action lawsuit, and they needed some help so Brian, my fiancé, volunteered to go. He took a few of the interns with him, and they've been there for a few weeks. My boss asked me if I wanted time off to fly down and see him for a few days, and naturally, I jumped at the opportunity. I missed him and hadn't seen him for so long." I feel myself rambling, so I take another deep breath to steady myself.

"So, short story long, I showed up to his hotel last night to surprise him and found him with one of his interns. He had her bent over the desk in the room and was giving her the business end of a deposition, if you know what I mean!" I snort, half at my punny joke and half to emphasize my point.

Vincent smirks a little at the comment. "I did not go to law school, but I can deduce what that statement means."

"I didn't even say a word to him; I just turned around and left the room. I was shocked and didn't even know what to do. He followed me and tried apologizing and giving every excuse in the book from 'it's not what you think,' to 'it's your fault because you haven't come to visit me here.' I just took the ring off and handed it back to him, er— maybe I threw it at him; I can't recall. We live together, so that's another nightmare I have to figure out when I get back. I haven't told my sister or my boss."

Shock registers on his otherwise passive face. "You win. Not that it's a competition, that sounds rude, but fuck. You've had one shitty day. Not to pry, but did you suspect anything?"

7

"I wouldn't say I suspected infidelity but...the truth is I was settling. I think I was aware of that; I just didn't want to admit it. When I met Brian, things were great; we were young and in love and all that. But now..." I feel my words slurring together. I am wildly out of character at this point. Miss Type-A, always in control and uptight, is letting it all out to a complete stranger. I rub my hand over my face, most likely smearing my makeup. "I mean, I still love him...it just fucking sucks to put your trust and faith in someone and have this entire life planned out and they just throw you away for someone that 'didn't mean anything.'" I make sure to use dramatic air quotes to emphasize my point.

I look over at him as I shrug my shoulders in shame. He's unsure of what to say, but his eyes are sympathetic to my situation.

"I feel like a privileged asshole complaining about this stuff. I'm sorry."

He reaches out and brushes a stray section of hair behind my ear. It startles me, and I'm sure the emotion shows on my face as he pulls his hand back quickly.

"I'm sorry, I hate seeing a beautiful woman cry." His eyes drop to my lips briefly before he turns back to face his drink.

"Well, Alison, you do have a right to be unhappy about where your life is going; privileged or not, we all deserve happiness. The important thing is, if you are unhappy, you have to be willing to be uncomfortable to change it. Otherwise, you'll be stuck in the same situation complaining about the same things over and over. The big question now is, what are you going to do?"

I let out a deep sigh as I look up toward the ceiling. "I don't have a fucking clue, Vincent." I can feel my phone vibrate in my pocket again as the bartender sends me over another dirty vodka martini. I nod a thank you and reach into my pocket. "Finally! My flight is scheduled to depart in the next thirty-five minutes; looks like my delay was cut short. My section should be boarding soon."

Vincent checks his watch and then pulls out his phone. "Lucky you. Looks like my flight is still delayed with no scheduled departure."

I throw a few bills on the bar top and stand up to gather my things.

8

"Thanks for being my airport therapist. It was nice to talk so freely to a complete stranger, admitting things that I haven't even said aloud to myself."

"Happy to listen. It was lovely meeting you, Alison Ryder."

He gives me a crooked smile as he reaches into his pocket again and pulls out his business card.

"In case you need someone to drink an overpriced martini and have another therapy session with when you get back to Chicago." I smile and take the card from him; our fingertips briefly touch, sending a current through my body. Just as I turn to walk away, he pipes back up.

"Oh, and if you're looking to completely uproot your life, I'm looking for an assistant." I laugh, unsure if he's serious, but a little intrigued at the idea. I won't lie: the thought of jet setting around Europe for several weeks on someone else's dime sounds like a dream job...especially if it means spending time with him every day.

"Thanks again, Vincent. It was great meeting you. I hope you get everything sorted and can find a replacement assistant soon. Best of luck on the acquisition!"

I grab my suitcase and make my way toward my gate. I know I just met the man, but weirdly I feel a little sad walking away from him. A small part also questions if he really just hit on me after telling him I found my fiancé cheating. The thought of Brian makes my stomach churn...I feel like a piece of shit too. I'm still coasting on the realization that my six-year relationship is over and my heart's broken while I'm fantasizing about a complete stranger.

I am technically now homeless and single...I just need to get on my flight and let my thoughts marinate in the vodka now sloshing around my brain.

VINCENT

I was two glasses of scotch in when I saw the petite blonde come barreling into the airport bar. She was breathtaking and looked as though she were ready to rip a few heads off. She didn't seem to notice me as she waved the bartender over and ordered her dirty martini.

She looked a bit disheveled, but I could see from her fitted pencil skirt and silk blouse she had a taste for fashion and knew how to dress for her body. It was only a matter of minutes before the shark approached.

I watched as she handled her own like a pro. I have to admit; it was even a little intimidating to see such a gorgeous woman own her looks and not feel she owed anyone anything for it. I didn't feel a bit sorry for the overzealous, drunk asshole that though he could get to her with just an offer to buy her a drink. Guys like him give us all a bad name. A woman wants to feel important and special, like she's the only one in the room. I have a talent for it; I won't lie. I've never once struggled to get a woman to notice me, or into my bed.

I was more than a little curious to know what series of events brought her to this moment. Being that I was stuck at the airport for god knew how long, I figured it couldn't hurt to make small talk with a stranger. Especially someone as gorgeous as her.

"That was a pretty brutal rejection; you seemed well practiced at it though." I raised my glass to her and watched as the look of disgust melted off her face when she saw me. Yeah, I have that effect on women. I reached over and introduced myself to her, offering to swap stories.

I let my eyes drop from hers down her long, slender neck. She's delicate and smooth: the kind of woman you can't help but want to see beneath you gripping the sheets and calling out your name.

I listened intently as she described her day. My assistant quitting certainly didn't seem like that big of a deal once I listened to her detail how she just caught her fiancé cheating on her. While I couldn't relate to that situation, it was exactly why I preferred my "relationships" to be quick and easy...no emotions, no commitments, just sex. At least, that's what I told myself. I'd never considered anything more until I started watching everyone around me find 'the one.'

I wasn't sure what it was, but something about her intrigued me. Her beauty was something to be admired, but it wasn't that. She was driven and ambitious; she just needed a little guidance...someone to mentor her.

When I was her age, I was mentored by a man named Hershel Fitzsimmons; he was what they called a 'wolf of Wall Street.' Powerful and intimidating but never disrespectful or one to waste your time. He was direct and honest, and that bothered a lot of people, but it got him to the top of his financial game. I watched him be genuine and honest with his clients and partners over the years, and I knew that was the kind of man I wanted to be. I never wanted to betray the trust of the people who helped me build my success.

I pull out the pocket watch that Hershel left me when he died. He always told me, 'Never waste anyone's time because time is the only thing we can't get more of.' It's a constant reminder of how far I've come since the days when I was washing dishes in the back of an ancient diner to put myself through college and supplement my scholarship to Dartmouth. The road from New Hampshire to Chicago was a long one and seemed eternally uphill. The even longer road had been the one I'd gone down to get from being abandoned as a toddler with my nearly destitute grandparents by a drug addict of a mother, to being the fourth-richest person on the North American continent. It sure as hell hadn't been because I was timid and afraid to go after what I want. I'm a man who doesn't understand the word 'can't.'

I learned from a very early age that the only way I was going to get what I wanted in life was to go after it with wild abandon. I'd gone after my first hotel like a cheetah after a gazelle...nothing but pure determination, precision, and the realization that failure wasn't an option.

At twenty-five-years-old, I had talked enough investors into giving me money to buy a bankrupt hotel in the middle of Chicago's Magnificent Mile and renovate it, turning it into one of the most sought-after accommodations not only in Chicago, but all of North America. I put everything I had into making that happen, and my motto was, "Work hard, play even harder."

I knew what it was like to go to bed hungry, to not know if you'd have a roof over your head, to have nobody to depend on. The day I made my first thousand dollars, I promised myself I'd never take a single breath for granted again.

The cost of my constant dedication to building my business was a lack of personal relationships. I watched as my best friend Nate Baldwin had met and fell in love with his now-fiancée Elise, both of whom worked for my company. Nate as CFO and Elise as my in-house legal counsel. I love giving Nate a hard time about being completely pussy whipped, but the truth is I'm envious of him and what he has with Elise.

While we were working on our degrees at Dartmouth, I had watched him jump from date to date just as I had. Back then, we made bets with one another about who could get the most numbers in one night or could bring a girl back to our dorm the quickest. It's not like I set out to be a playboy asshole who never settled down, but somewhere along the way, life happened, and here I am.

I pull out my phone, typing in the name of the design firm she mentioned: Madeline Dwyer Designs. I flip through the images on the website, clearly a high-end establishment with several well-to-do clients in the Chicagoland area. I click on the 'our staff' link and scrolled down till I see a familiar face. There she is: Alison Ryder, associate designer.

I let my thumb hover over the number of the firm for just a brief second before dialing, I glance at my watch hoping I still catch someone in the office since it's almost six.

"Madeline Dwyer Designs, this is Tiffany speaking; how may I direct your call?"

"Hello, Tiffany. My name is Vincent Crawford. I'd like to speak with Madeline directly please."

"I'm sorry Mr. Crawford, do you have an appointment with Miss Dwyer?"

I'm not one for name dropping, but in a situation like this, I'm not above doing it either. "No, I don't, but I'm the owner and CEO of Castille Hotels. I'm looking to hire her firm to take on a massive contract to completely redesign several of my hotels."

"I—I'm sorry, Mr. Crawford, let me make sure she's in her office and I'll put you through."

I drum my fingers on the bar top as I wait to be patched through. Nate would give me hell right now if he knew what I was about to do.

ALISON

I chew nervously on my pen cap, reading and re-reading the text on my phone while I sit at my desk in my cramped office. I refocus, tossing the pen on my desk and twirling a long strand of my hair around my finger. I've been told over the years the habit is unbecoming and makes me look desperate and ditzy, but I always do it when I'm feeling particularly stressed.

"Knock, knock. You okay, Ali? You look like you've had about six espresso shots for breakfast." I look up to see my coworker Chloe smiling at me with a look of slight concern on her face.

"Yeah, yeah, I'm good. Great. Why, what's up?" My sad attempt at masking my anxiety is betrayed by how squeaky I sound.

I won't lie: the fact that I am always defending against the dumb blonde stereotype and that I'm the youngest junior designer at this firm has given me a bit of a chip on my shoulder, and I am determined to not let first impressions be last impressions. Sometimes it means I get a little too wrapped up in being the perfectionist I am. Like right now, for example. It also makes me second guess my abilities and confidence in my job. Something I hate greatly.

Chloe still stands in the doorway to my office with a look on her face, waiting for me to elaborate on why I'm so jumpy.

"I got a text from Madeline first thing this morning telling me she needed to speak with me. She's cleared her calendar and wants me to make it a priority."

Chloe glances at the watch on her arm. "And you're dragging ass because? It's almost nine-forty-five already; that's not exactly making it a priority to Madeline Dwyer."

"I know, I know. I'm just—avoiding it? What if I'm getting canned?"

Chloe's crossed arms drop to her sides. "You can't be serious, Alison. You are the best designer in this office besides Madeline. We all want to be you! You need to grow some balls and realize how amazing you are." She cocks her hip and points her finger in my direction with conviction.

Maybe she's right...I have worked my ass off to land my dream job, and I should be more confident in my abilities and judgment. I stand up sharply, smoothing the front of my shift dress and grabbing my iPad. "You know what? You're right! I am a professional, modern woman!"

I walk swiftly around my desk and high-five a laughing Chloe as I make my way confidently towards Madeline's office.

"That's right, girl! You got this; woot-woot!" Chloe calls after me as I raise a fist in the air.

Right before I round the corner, I turn to face her again, "Oh, and I'll be grabbing those last few boxes from your place this weakened. Thanks again for letting me stay with you. Tell Stan he's a trooper for putting up with two women for that long. I owe you a lot of wine."

Madeline Dwyer is everything I want to be. She's cool, calm, completely put together, and knows her business like no other person in the city of Chicago. She started this business on her own in her twenties, while she was still in college, no less, and has run it on her own ever since, rising to become one of the premier design firms in the country.

This firm is her baby, and because of that, she values the people she hires; nobody gets in unless Madeline hand-picks them. It's probably the reason that Madeline is still single well into her forties despite the plethora of men who try to work their way into her life.

I feel my heart in my throat. I try replaying Chloe's words in my head over and over, but my nerves are starting to get the better of me again. I wait patiently outside of Ms. Dwyer's office for her executive assistant to summon me into the largest office in the building: one with a corner view that looks out over the whole city...naturally. It makes the room that I work out of look like a closet. Those are the perks when you run an entire company instead of just being a newbie designer in a huge firm. It also lights a fire under my ass to work my up.

For all my drive and ambition, the truth is, I'm still new to this game. I am the youngest designer in the firm, barely older than the interns. I was one of those interns just a few years ago. I loved interning here. Madeline gave us every opportunity to learn from her, and I jumped at it. I was burning the candle at both ends in those days, but it paid off. I received an offer letter before I even graduated from college.

"Ms. Dwyer will see you now." Her assistant Sophie doesn't even look up from her desk as she hangs up the phone and calls me into the office. I push open the large door, swallowing to get the knot in my throat as I walk into the room. Madeline is sitting in the chair behind the desk with a folder in hand, her glasses resting at the end of her nose as she studies whatever paperwork is inside.

"Have a seat, Alison." She puts the folder down, grabbing her glasses off their perch and uses them to point to the chair opposite her. I slide into place, trying not to look as nervous as I am. My legs feel like a baby deer's as I lower myself to the chair.

"Morning, Ms. Dwyer." I can hear my voice wanting to shake, but I fight back and refuse to let it come out of my throat. *I am a strong, confident, modern woman who is talented, driven, and deserves success.*

"Morning." She picks up the file and passes it over the desk to me. I reach for it, opening it and reading the words printed on the title page. *Castille Hotels* is emblazoned across it in what I recognize as

Madeline's careful and ornate handwriting. I flip through it for a moment before looking back up at my boss in confusion.

"I don't understand. Is this a new project?"

"We have a new client, as you can see from the information in that folder. Castille Hotels is in the market for a designer to plan renovations in several of their locations. They contacted me the other day, and I thought this might be a good chance for you to prove yourself."

Her voice is calm and even, betraying nothing of what is going on behind the gray-blue of her eyes. Madeline's hard to read on a good day, and this morning caught me entirely off guard. I can feel my eyes growing a little wide, despite my determination not to show Madeline how off-kilter all of this has thrown me.

"I don't understand. I'm almost done with the staging designs for the new Adam Mitchell furniture store you gave me last week, but it's just the initial designs. There's still so much to do."

"Don't worry about that," she says with a casual flick of her wrist. "I already spoke with Chloe, and she was more than happy to take that project over for you. I also called the client, and they were happy to work with Chloe again. She helped them years ago when they opened their flagship store."

I nod as she speaks, still trying to come to terms with the fact that she just handed me the opportunity of a lifetime. I take a deep, calming breath. "I mean…this is a huge job, and if you think I'm up to the challenge, then I'm going to be up to the challenge."

I look from the folder to my boss, steeling my features and owning the fact that I am capable. In reality, I want to jump on top of the chair and scream with excitement. Most designers have to work a decade before they are handed an opportunity like this.

"Fair enough. I wouldn't have offered you the job if I didn't think you were up to it." Once again, Madeline's stoic features give nothing away. "It's going to require a lot of travel. Mr. Crawford has already said it will all be at his own expense. You'll be using his private jet and staying at his hotels." If she considered how intimidating this is for me, she certainly doesn't give anything away.

"So when do I start?" I close the folder and place it on my lap.

17

There will be a lot of research to do, and I plan to start as soon as I walk out of this room and back to my office. There isn't a chance in hell I am going to screw this up by going into it unprepared. Looks like my nights and weekends just got booked up for several weeks.

"Right now, but your first meeting with the client isn't until tomorrow at his headquarters on Michigan Avenue. You have an appointment at ten. The address is in the folder. Sophie has sent you an invite on your calendar, and she's given you access to all of the folders on the network." She nods towards the door, bending to pick up a pen from the desktop and jot something down on a piece of paper. "Now go get started. As of right now, this is your only account. Make it count, Alison."

"Yes, ma'am. I'll get right on it," I say, standing up and leaving the room quickly, pulling out my cell phone out to immediately start searching for information on the company. I barely make it out of Madeline's office and around the corner before I let out a squeak of excitement and run toward the elevator bank.

I've heard of Castille Hotels before. You'd have to be living under a rock not to know who they are. Luxury hotels that are found on nearly every continent on the face of the planet are hard to miss. When you live in the city where the brand was founded, it is even harder to have never heard of them. I know less about the owner of the company, but a quick search will fix that.

My breath catches in my throat as I click on Google images. Holy shit, it's the guy from the airport bar! *Mr. Crawford,* Madeline's voice rings in my head. I scurry back to my office and grab my purse, rummaging through it frantically until I find what I'm looking for. I pull out the business card he'd handed me and flip it over. There on the back in gold embossing is the emblem for Castille Hotels. I must have been too inebriated to have noticed it.

Vincent Crawford is only thirty-six years old, but he is already a freaking billionaire. I take a moment to look at his face in the photos; the airport bar was dark and didn't do him justice. He's gorgeous, actual perfection. The kind of guy who would make you abandon everything you ever believed in for one kiss. His thick, dark hair flops carelessly over one eye in one photo, his sparkling teeth set perfectly against his plump lips.

I scroll through his Wikipedia page. Apparently, he didn't come from money. Everything he has is self-made. There's pretty much zero detail on his actual childhood or family; most of it is details about his business and crazy personal life. I flip back to the Google images page and see a string of photos of Vincent with models and actresses draped across his arms, never the same one twice.

I sit back heavily in my chair as I take in the photos of him. "I was definitely drunk to have no not realized his level of fuck-me-side-ways-hotness." I roll my eyes as I flip through the photos. "So cliché." The other photos are of him skiing down mountains in Europe, skydiving, jumping off a bridge in Australia with nothing but a bungee rope tied to his ankles.

"Failed Tinder date?" Chloe reappears in my office doorway with a smile on her face.

"No, this new guy I'm going to be working for." I flip the phone around, so she can see what I'm looking at. She steps into the room and grabs my phone, flipping through the images.

"Daaaaamn, he is one tasty morsel!" She whistles as she admires a shirtless photo of him on a beach in the south of France.

"A little too predictable don't you think? Models ten years younger than him and million-dollar cars." I wrinkle my nose in fake disgust. Is this really the same guy I met at the airport? He seemed so different... so normal, unlike all these pictures.

"Someone sounds jealous...or intimated, maybe? Congrats on the job, by the way. I told you you'd be fine."

"So you knew? Thanks for taking on the Mitchell file, by the way." I'm tempted to bring up the fact that I met the man at the airport, but then I worry how that will look. I meet this random guy at the airport, then he hires the firm, and I just happen to get the job?

Chloe has been working at the firm for close to ten years; she just solidified her place as Madeline's top designer and is now managing the interns. And she was my knight in shining armor that let me bunk with her for a few weeks until I found a new apartment.

19

"Yeah, Madeline ran it by me. I thought it would be the perfect opportunity to get your feet wet. And no worries about the Mitchell file; that's what I have interns for," she says with a wink before heading back down the hall.

I sit back in my chair, not letting the fact that Mr. Sex-on-a-stick-airport-fantasy is actually kind of a playboy and not exactly the kind of man I'd date. Maybe Chloe is right; I am judging this guy. Besides, he's a job. I wasn't hired to date him; I was hired to work for him.

My idea of a wild Saturday night is getting Chinese takeout to eat while binge-watching old B-rated horror movies or catching up on work. While I don't expect to spend any personal time with the client, I like to have an idea of the person and their interests; it helps me get a feel for their sense of style and design.

This is how I once again wind up in my office with a strand of hair wound nervously around my finger. My first meeting with Vincent was less than impressive. I was a half-drunk bumbling mess. That is not the image I want to portray to my clients. My future at my firm and in the industry most definitely depends on my performance on this assignment. If it works out, this is going on my resume for the rest of my career. If it doesn't, I am likely to be blacklisted from working for anyone in Chicago for the next decade.

I catch my bottom lip in between my teeth and bite down hard before letting out a long sigh. There is a lot on the line with this job. I have to keep my head down, mind open, and make sure the client is happy. I don't need to be best friends with the man; I don't have to like him. I just have to decorate his hotels and make one hell of an impression. This could be the launching pad for me to not only solidify my name in the design world, but to make connections that later help me establish my own firm.

Picking up a notebook and pen, I jot down a few quick notes from image searches of the list of locations I'm starting with. Eventually, the entire chain is going to be redecorated, but for now, they are starting on their oldest locations, needing to get them up to date.

It has been ten years since he purchased and started his first location here in Chicago. It is past due for an update, and I already have a few ideas. I need to look through the location and get a feel for the way things work and flow in the hotel. The decor needs to be more than just beautiful. It needs to be comfortable and functional as well.

A lot of people could make a room look amazing. Looks most certainly aren't everything. Madeline understands that better than most. If a room isn't usable, if in the end, it isn't a space someone can feel comfortable working or living in, then it is a failure. Interior design is a balance between art and function, everything that I love, and in the end, it is the space itself that tells me what it needs.

I finish jotting down some notes, glancing at the clock; it is lunchtime, and there isn't much more I can do while my stomach is completely empty. I've not only done a thorough search of all the material that the internet can provide about both Vincent Crawford and his company, but I've filled my iPad with inspirational photos and colors that I can share with him during our meeting tomorrow. The rest is going to fall into place when I take a tour of the property and get a feel for the layout.

I click back to the open Google images tab and scroll through more photos of him. I think back to the airport when he reached up and brushed a strand of hair back. I let my eyes close for a moment and wonder what would have happened if I had leaned into his hand. Maybe we would have shared a few passionate, secretive kisses before I dashed off to my flight. Suddenly my eyes shoot open, and I can feel my face blushing. Thank god things didn't go that far; I can't imagine walking into his office tomorrow with that being our last moment together. I need to stay focused!

I grab my phone, tapping out a quick text to my little sister Janelle.

Hey, J. Want to grab a bite to eat? I've got a lot to talk to you about.

Janelle is a lot more than just my baby sister; she is the person that I trust most in the world. The two of us have been best friends since childhood. It is Janelle that keeps me sane and grounded most days. We are opposites—night and day, that's for sure. Janelle's light-hearted take on the world is the thing that balances out my serious moods and insane focus. She is the live-in-the-moment, don't-take-the-world-too-seriously type. Something I struggle to embrace. If anyone can help me relax a little, it is going to be Janelle.

My phone goes off almost immediately. It is a Monday. Janelle should be in class for the next half-hour, but of course, there is always the chance that she skipped it and will be free for the rest of the day, or that she is simply replying from the back of the lecture hall.

Yeah, babe. Meet me at our restaurant in half an hour?

My initial reaction is to tell her to either pay attention or get her ass to class, but one thing I've learned over the years with Janelle is she's going to do whatever the hell she wants. I smile to myself and type out a response.

Great. See you there. xo

I grab my bag and make my way to the front desk, telling the receptionist I am going to lunch and if anyone comes looking for me to send me a text. In all likelihood, no one is going to be looking for me, but I feel guilty for skipping out on work for a long lunch break, no matter how much I might need it. I am going to be out of the office a lot in the next few weeks though. There is no telling when I'll be back in once this project kicks off, and all my work can be done from home.

I keep reminding myself that Vincent Crawford is my only job. I make my way to the closest train station to catch the L and head off to the bistro that Janelle and I love. This is going to be a long job and a once-in-a-lifetime opportunity, and I can't wait to tell her about it.

* * *

"Okay, I've got a garden egg white omelet with a side of fruit?" My sister raises her hand as the waiter smiles and places it in front of her.

"And the cookies and cream pancakes with extra whipped cream and a side of bacon and hash browns?" I raise my hand even though I am the only other person at the table.

The waiter gives me a bit of a shocked looked as he sets my plates down. Annoyed by his perceived judgment, I snap back, "I'm stressed, okay."

"I'm sorry about that. Thank you so much; it all looks delicious," Janelle says to the young man as he scurries back to the kitchen.

"Okay, Alison, time to put your big-girl panties on and stop scaring people. Technically, you dumped Brian; just saying. Plus it's been a few months; why is this happening all the sudden? Eat your fifteen-thousand-calorie lunch and get your game face on because we are going to brainstorm how to get your life on track and how to get over that sack of shit."

"What are you even talking about? This has nothing to do with that asshole. I'm work stressed."

"Oh, sorry. Tell me what's going on; you said you had a lot to talk about?" she says, quickly changing the subject.

"Yeah, so...this is kind of a crazy story, but I met this guy at the airport in Dallas while my flight was delayed." I launch into the entire story, trying not to elaborate on the fact that he looked like a walking wet dream.

"Oh my god, Ali, that's amazing! Congrats!" She lifts her glass of orange juice to cheers me. "Now let's get back to that part where you said he's handsome. Are we talking handsome as in older man that could be our dad's age or handsome as in he'll fuck you until you call him daddy?"

I roll my eyes; I knew she'd pick up on that detail. "Honestly, Elle, he's the kind of guy that only talks to me because he's trapped in an airport bar and bored out of his mind...and one thousand percent the fuck-you-until-you-call-him-daddy type," I say, pulling out my phone to show her the pictures.

She gives me a little smirk. "So, wait. What are the odds that you meet this guy and then, bam, he hires your firm? Did you tell him you worked there?" She reaches for the phone before slamming her hand down on the table with a straight up screech. "LORD HAVE MERCYYYYY!"

I nod, swallowing the large bite of pancakes I just snarfed down as I snatch the phone back from her and give a polite, apologetic smile to people around us. "We're in public, Elle!" I scold as she looks around without a care.

"But yes, I casually mentioned it. I didn't think he was listening that closely, but I guess he was. Anyway, worked out in my favor that Madeline put me on the contract."

Elle's eyes shrink to slits. "Riiiight, she just happened to put you on the contract. Twenty bucks he called asking specifically for you."

"Cheers to me! I am going to kick ass on this job!" We both raise our glasses, but I can't help but wonder if that's true.

4

VINCENT

My office overlooks The Loop, directly across from the first hotel I bought ten years ago. It's one of my favorite things to look at in this city. To me, it shows that no matter where you come from, if you put your mind to it, you can achieve unbelievable success.

"Mr. Crawford, there's a Miss Alison Ryder here to see you from Madeline Dwyer Designs," my temporary assistant says. A huge smile spreads across my face. I am excited to see her again, curious if she'll be shocked to see me or if she Googled me when she received the assignment from her boss.

"Send her in, Gretchen."

I run my hands through my hair and settle back into reading the document laid out across my desk: a deal for buying a location in Toronto that needs updating and upgrading.

Toronto is the perfect location for another of my hotels. It is close to the Canadian Tire Motorsports Park, and I've been looking for a new place to house some of my cars. Not to mention the number of businesses and events in Toronto. It is just screaming for me to add one of my luxury hotels, even if the competition in the area is steep.

One of the older hotel owners was shopping for a buyer to liquidate some of his assets, and I had been the first person his agent had called. I always put out feelers in the area before I establish a new location. I've learned over the years that it's easier to flip an older property than to build from the ground up, especially with luxury lines. I pay good money to be told when something like this comes available in certain cities. That's why I hired Madeline's firm. I have expanded at a rapid rate over the last several years, and it's time to flip the properties I've acquired.

I hear the office door open and close before looking up to see Alison enter the room. She looks different from what I remember, younger actually, and even more drop-dead gorgeous than I registered at the time. Her blonde hair is pulled into a tight knot at her neck, and it is safe to say that not a hair is out of place. Her clothes are immaculate, from the freshly starched white button-down to the red pencil skirt that matches the heels that grace her feet.

I've seen more than my fair share of 'hot.' I've had it in my bed more times than I care to count. Alison has a different look, a determined look that says she has something prove. I can see it in the shrewdness in her gray-blue eyes and in the way she holds herself.

I push myself up from my chair and walk around the desk, offering the young woman my hand.

"Good morning, Miss...well, I'm afraid they didn't tell me your name," I joke. I raise an eyebrow but don't even try to keep the corners of my mouth from curling up into a smirk. I am already amused by the look on her face as she takes my hand, and I can't help but notice her eyes drop from my hand to my crotch. I grin; I would love to know exactly what is going through that pretty head of hers. She realizes I noticed and her eyes dart up to mine as her cheeks blaze bright red.

"Pleasure to see you again, Mr. Crawford. I see you got a new admin?" She smiles with amusement as she shakes my hand before dropping it, moving to hold the tablet she's brought with her against her chest. I still feel a charge of energy when she touches my hand; I'm curious if she feels it too. If so, she gives nothing away. She looks like an honor student on her first day of school. Already prepared to be the teacher's pet and ace the class. I motion for her to take a seat in one of the chairs across from my desk.

"Just a temp for now. Job is still open if you're interested?"

"I'll consider it." She gives me a pathetic grin before continuing, "I have to admit, I was a little shocked when my boss called me in and told me that you were looking for an interior designer. I understand you're looking to update several of your hotel locations?" She opens the iPad and begins to flip through files.

"Well, when you mentioned that you worked for a prestigious firm in Chicago, it reminded me that my old assistant had been working to find us a designer to redo several of our locations. I figured it was a sign we were meant to meet." I flash her my best charming grin, but she doesn't seem to take the bait. I want to ask her why she seems so different from that night at the airport...was it the booze? Maybe the whirlwind of all of the events that had taken place that day? Gone is the carefree woman who wasn't afraid to tell off the drunk dude who tried hitting on her, and in her place is a stoic, if not demure, young woman.

"Ms. Dwyer thought I'd be a good fit for the job. I must say, it's a very large and in-depth project. I'm excited to get started working with you." She doesn't miss a beat, keeping her calm exterior as she speaks. I don't tell her that I asked for her specifically. I think the owner was reluctant to send over someone so fresh, but I demanded she be the one I work with.

Straight to business: that's how she is going to be. I have to admit, her uptight demeanor amuses me more than it should. I may have to break the ice a little.

"Pleasure to be working with you." I walk away from her and over to the bar on the far side of the office. "Can I get you a drink? Vodka martini perhaps?"

If straight to business is what she wants, it is the last thing she is going to get. I take my time pouring myself a shot of aged whiskey before turning around to face her.

"No, thank you, Mr. Crawford. I don't drink very often, and not before noon."

"Only at airport bars with strangers."

I can see the lack of enthusiasm on her face.

"Well, I'd hate to have you break your 'never before noon' rule so I guess we can pick that back up later." I throw a wink at her as I walk back over to the desk with a low chuckle.

"Thanks again for keeping me company at the airport. I must say, I appreciated our encounter and was sad it ended so soon."

Her posture is stiff as she pulls on the hem of her skirt. "Mr. Crawford, did you call my firm and ask for me specifically to work on this contract?"

I was waiting for this question. "Yes." She stares at me, blinking rapidly.

"Why?"

"Why not? I was in need of a designer, and when you mentioned your job, I took the chance."

"Yes, that makes sense, but I am merely a junior designer. Why not have one of our senior associates handle this? Why did you ask for me?" I can tell there's an unspoken question there.

"Because I want you." I can see her swallow hard. "I liked your tenacity when I met you, and I only want you touching my assets." It's a cheap innuendo, but it works, as she shifts again in her seat.

Working with her is going to be a trip; lucky for her, I welcome a good challenge. I'm sure Alison did her due diligence and Googled me. I'm aware of what pops up though I don't make it a habit to research myself anymore. It is only a half story. I always love when someone thinks they know who I am based off something they read or saw about me online, not that I feel any judgement from her. Perhaps my own insecurities getting the better of me.

Keeping half of myself secret is one of my greatest pleasures. Let them all think I'm a typical playboy and daredevil looking for my next conquest or adrenaline rush. I know the truth, and those closest to me know it as well. Something inside me wants to let Alison know the truth, too, but if she is going to assume she can learn about me from what she reads online, then I will let her have her little illusions for now.

"Well, thank you then for allowing me this opportunity. I know our initial meeting was very unorthodox and I was completely out of sorts, so I don't want you to think that is the kind of approach I will be taking with this position."

"Oh trust me, Alison, I don't doubt your abilities for a second. In fact, I'm confident you can handle any position I put you in."

Two seconds after seeing her again and I am already picturing those red heels up by my ears and my name tumbling from her full lips...*fuck me, this is going to be hard.*

5

ALISON

I stare at myself in the floor-length mirror, smoothing out my outfit and making sure it isn't stuck in any ill-fitting spots. I know it's a silly thing to enjoy about a job, but I love being able to express myself a little through fashion. I meet with clients pretty regularly, so of course, it is encouraged. I slick on a pinky-nude gloss to finish off my polished look.

I have an entire zoo of butterflies in my stomach as my Uber makes its way over to Castille Hotels corporate office. I'm always nervous meeting first-time clients, but they usually aren't men that can make me throw my moral code out the window with one look. Not to mention, the last time I saw Mr. Crawford, my hormones shot into overdrive and I felt the need to squeeze my thighs together for some sweet relief.

Pulling up to the building, my nerves only heighten. An imposing edifice with Castille Hotels emblazoned in gold letters across the top. I can't help but wonder…compensating for something?

I take a deep breath and shake off my nerves as I enter the building and make my way to the reception desk. "Uh, hi, my name is Alison Ryder. I have an appointment this morning with Mr. Vincent Crawford."

The petite redhead behind the desk doesn't miss a beat. "Please sign in on the iPad, Miss Ryder." She motions to the one mounted to her left. "Here is your visitor's badge; please wear it in a visible spot for the duration of your visit. Mr. Crawford's office is on the top floor; you're going to want to go through the turnstiles behind you and take the first bank of elevators to your right. Once you reach the top floor, take an immediate left, and a Mrs. Windmeyer will be there to show you to Mr. Crawford's office." She gives me a curt smile and nod as if to signal that the conversation is over.

"Thank you," I say as I finish signing in, then turn around to follow her directions. My heels click on the marble floor as I follow a group of employees to the elevators. By the time I reach the top floor, I am the last person on board. I nervously step out and look to my left to see a small, white-haired lady waiving me towards her desk. I look around the floor as I make my way toward Mrs. Windmeyer.

"Hello, Miss Ryder; lovely to meet you." She stands and gives me a hearty handshake for such a small woman. "You have such a cute figure; I remember when I looked like that." She winks at me as she ushers me toward the massive solid oak doors of Mr. Crawford's office. She knocks as she pushes the door open. "Mr. Crawford, there's a Miss Ryder here for your appointment."

I turn and thank her for the lovely compliment as I enter Vincent's office. It is more in line with what I pictured than the sterile outside. Everything looks as if it were handpicked for him. Rich mahogany, deep jewel tones, and gold accents surround the room. It is opulent and classy without being gaudy. Clearly, he paid a pretty penny for this office.

Vincent stands and walks around his desk to greet me; I hadn't realized the first time we met how impressive his stature was...just like the building he had picked for his business. It isn't just that he is uncharacteristically tall or built, but the way he carries himself commands your attention. His three-piece Savile Row suit is impeccably tailored and for some unknown, godforsaken reason, my eyes drop to his crotch!

I knew what I was getting myself into when I entered Vincent's office. At least, I thought I did. I was a little unprepared for what Vincent Crawford was like in real life. Offering me a drink at ten in the morning threw me off kilter. I was almost kicking myself for not taking it when he went back to his desk. But then again, what kind of impression would that have made?

He isn't the same guy I met at the airport, but then again, I was entirely out of character then as well. Maybe he was, and I was too wrapped up in my pity party and alcohol to clearly remember the events. One thing is for sure though: he's even hotter than I remember. He has to be well over six feet, and his silky hair and piercing eyes are a deadly combo. Part of me wants to rip that expensive suit off his rock-hard body and pick up where we left off at the airport.

"So, I took the liberty of doing some research on your hotel chain." I pull two folders out of my bag, handing him one and keeping the other. There is a lot of detail with this job to get through, so setting expectations with him and getting him to focus is paramount to success.

"I included some of my previous projects in that file, a small portfolio, if you will, of my design career. I'm sure you have your ideas and visions for this renovation; just think of me as your professional guide in this journey."

Vincent doesn't say anything as he flips through the documents, glancing over them quickly. "Well, Miss Ryder, I'm very impressed. I think you went above and beyond in your preparation for this meeting. I get the sense that this is how you operate in all facets of life?"

"Uh, yeah...yes. You could say I'm a bit of an overachiever. My fiancé calls me a very organized and compassionate psychopath," I say as a nervous laugh escapes my lips.

"Fiancé? You two have mended things?"

"Er...ex-fiancé. Sorry, I'm still not used to saying that." I fidget with the file. It's been a few months since I ended things with Brian, but that word still creeps in now and then.

"No need to apologize. I probably shouldn't have inquired anyway; none of my business." There is a moment of awkward silence before he places the portfolio on the table between us.

"I suppose you'll want me to start here in Chicago?" I shoot him a look across the desk, then glance back down at my file, making sure to keep my voice and demeanor strictly business.

"Yes, Chicago first, then New York, Denver, Hawaii, and Iceland. Maybe a few other locations after that. We can work out travel plans as we go, I suppose. I'll be sure to have my secretary copy you on all travel arrangements."

I jot down the list and avoid letting my eyes go wide at the last few destinations. It wasn't everyone who could say that they were going to get paid to go and stay in a luxury hotel at any of those destinations as part of their work. It was one of the perks of the job, in this case. Though something about the last sentence catches me off guard.

"We?" I stop typing and glance up at Vincent, narrowing my eyes. "Does that mean you'll be coming with me, Mr. Crawford?"

I hold my breath, hoping the answer is no. That would make this job so much easier than it is shaping up to be, but something tells me I'm not going to get the answer I am looking for.

"Well, that is the plan." The chuckle in his voice is clear. He isn't even trying to hide it this time.

"Well then..." I clear my throat again and try to take the surprise out of my reply. "I suppose we're going to be working together for a long while."

This is going to take an adjustment. I already feel like an adolescent with her first schoolyard crush sitting in his office. Sneaking glances at the way he's rolled his sleeves up to expose his defined forearms or the sharp cut of his jawline. I had hoped the traveling would come as a stress reliever with all of the extensive work this contract includes, but now I'll be an anxious mess with my guard up the entire time.

"I promise not to be too much of a boss, Alison. I'm sure you know that I'm a fan of having a good time. Or didn't you read that about me in all of your research?" He gestures towards the tablet in my lap. He is mocking me now, judging from the tone of voice and the look in his eye. As frustrating as he is, I keep my composure and give him the fakest smile I can muster.

"I'm sure we'll get along famously, Mr. Crawford." I put emphasis on the Mr. It doesn't escape my notice that he refused to use the same formality with me. I'm not about to let him think I am comfortable around him by calling him Vincent; this relationship needs boundaries.

"Oh, I'm certain of it." He shoots me another seductive grin, running his hand through his vibrant hair. Why does he have to be so good looking? It would have been a lot easier to hate him if he weren't so disarming.

The photos online don't do the playful light in his eyes justice, or the way his face twitches involuntarily into that smile that makes my core clench. If I could kick myself, I would. That little voice inside that keeps my head on straight is screaming at me to stop lusting and stay focused. I just need to listen.

"So, I have some ideas I'd like to discuss with you about each of the hotels along with this file. Overall, they have a similar feel, but I want each of them to have their own details. The colors and decor should match the city that they're located in. Some of the buildings are historic, and it would be a shame to lose that history. It's going to be vital for you to visit each hotel and the surrounding cities. Each of them should feel like a luxurious but integral part of the city they're in." His face lights up as he speaks about his hotels; I can feel the passion in the tone of his voice.

"What would be perfect for Chicago is going to be ridiculous in Iceland and so on. I know I've thrown a lot at you this morning but for the moment, do you have any questions?" He raises an eyebrow. The idea of creating custom designs for each location is exciting, and the fact that he seems to have a clear vision for each one is promising and should make my job easier.

"Just one. When would you like to head over to the first hotel?" I put my focus back on the tablet in my lap, opening it to the calendar to thumb through my appointments, ready to put in a date that is going to work with his schedule. In the end, I am at his disposal.

"Why not right now?" He stands up while gesturing toward his office door.

"Oh, uh...ok."

I was expecting him to suggest something later in the week. Maybe him giving me the contact information to get in touch with the hotel manager to make an appointment. Instead, he's grabbing his suit jacket from the coat rack in the corner and shrugging it on over his shoulders while I scramble to gather my things.

He glances back at me while I'm still stuck in the chair, working to gather my items and place them strategically in my shoulder bag.

"Are you coming?" The look on his face is simultaneously annoying and enchanting. I scramble up from my seat, rushing over to join him.

"Of course, Mr. Crawford. You'll have to excuse me. I wasn't expecting you to want to get started right this minute." I follow him out of the door and to the elevator bank across from his office without a word from his secretary we pass on the way.

Maybe that's what working for this man means. You have to roll with the punches and be ready to fly by the seat of your pants, ready to jump off a bridge or out of an airplane at any second. I had hoped all my research would keep me one step ahead of Vincent Crawford, and I feel like I am already failing miserably.

"Starting today is not a problem, is it? Did you have somewhere else you needed to be?" The elevator dings and opens smoothly, almost soundlessly, in front of us. He places his hand on my lower back, ushering me into the box. His fingertips feel like they're going to burn through my shirt.

I shake my head as if that will help, stepping aside to let him hit the button for the ground floor. His arm brushes against my shoulder as I stand next to him. It's not enough that he's rich and powerful, but his looming stature and confidence seem to permeate the entire space.

"No, sir. You are my only focus until this job is complete." I almost hate to admit it to him, but he ought to know that the firm is putting as much effort as possible into his project.

"Oh?" I can hear the smirk in his voice without bothering to look over at his face. "Well, I'm flattered, but I'm certain you have something else to take your focus, at least during your free time."

There is a question there without him asking it. No, there isn't much else to take up my focus or time. I have a few friends, my sister being the main person in my life. I don't have a dog or a cat, not even a house plant that is going to wither while I am away. It is depressing to admit it. Now that I am single, I have all the time in the world.

Maybe he is trying to find out some more info on the ex-fiancé situation. I had completely forgotten that I confided in him about that. I can feel a red blush creeping up my neck at the memory.

"I'm free to travel wherever and whenever, Mr. Crawford, and trust me when I say that there's nothing that's going to be a distraction from my work. I take my job very seriously, and I want to reassure you that I will be fully dedicated to this project."

I keep my focus on the doors of the elevator and am more than a little relieved when they open. Being that close to Vincent Crawford had been more than I was prepared to handle.

"Well, in that case, I can't wait to use you to your fullest capabilities," he says as the doors open and I trip, spilling my belongings all over the floor and falling right into his arms.

6

VINCENT

I reach my arms out just in time as Alison catapults out of the elevator. Her bag and papers scatter across the floor as my right hand grabs her side, and my left hand lands squarely on her right breast.

"Oh my god, are you okay?" I ask as she scrambles to regain her balance and adjust her top and skirt. I quickly pull my hand back as we both look down at its resting place.

"Yes, sorry, I think my heel got caught on the space there." She's clearly embarrassed as bends down to gather her things.

"Here let me help you." I pick up the papers that flew out of her bag and hand them back to her.

"Shall we?" I reach out my arm to her, trying to make light of the situation.

"I'm sure I can manage it; thanks though." An exasperated smile spreads across her face as we make our way from the elevator and out of my office to the hotel lobby across the street.

"I love this hotel, even if it is starting to show its age," I say as we push through the large glass revolving door and into the grand lobby area. I can see her taking it all in, her mouth hanging open a bit as she spins in a circle.

"I have a confession; I've never actually never been inside here," she says with hesitation.

"Well, lucky for you, you have an excellent tour guide." I lean in a little closer, placing my fingertips against the small of her back.

"The lobby is beautiful in a classical way. The partially tiled floors in Italian marble and carpet are a bit dated, as you can tell. I'm also not the biggest fan of the heavy, floor-to-ceiling drapes or the rich velvet that seems to drown this place." She nods as I speak, her eyes dancing around the room while she takes photos with her iPad.

"Honestly, the bones of this hotel and lobby are magnificent. The dark, imposing reception area is a tad overwhelming and could be a little intimidating to guests," she says, dragging her hand along the smooth wood. I watch her dainty fingertips skitter over the desk and nearby pillar, imagining what it would feel like to have her wine-colored nails dragging across my bare chest.

What doesn't always meet the eye of the observer, but I notice, are the distressed carpets and upholstery. The carpet is worn from foot traffic, and the colors belong in the decade they were picked out in. Other people might not see it, but I have an eye for detail in my hotels, and it is clear Alison is on the same page.

I watch as she works furiously, taking notes on her tablet and using a stylus to sketch something here and there as we walk around the lobby without speaking. She doesn't need me next to her, but I don't want to walk away. She is in her element, and it is fascinating to watch.

"What's going through that beautiful head of yours?" I lean over her shoulder to see what she is sketching as she chews her bottom lip.

"You know, I work better without someone in my space. Feel free to go about your day; I'll reach out if I need something, Mr. Crawford," she says dismissively.

She's on edge. She gives off tension with every word she says. Just the tone of her voice tells me everything I need to know, but it is fun to watch her get flustered by my questions.

I raise my hands and step away from her, watching her wander off, discovering the nooks and crannies of the hotel for herself. I lean back into a column to watch her; women like her always let part of themselves out for the world to see when they really love something, and it is clear that she loves her job.

She is poking her head behind the curtains to study the architecture of the windows, leaning down to study the patterns in the marble floor and columns up close, and furiously jotting things down with the stylus that never leaves her right hand. There is no way I am going to interrupt her again.

"Observing the interior designer in her natural habitat?"

Nate walks up behind me, startling me out of my focused attention on Alison and back into the real world.

"Sorry, old man, I didn't mean to surprise you."

"No apologies necessary. I was just lost in thought." I turn my attention back to Alison, who is sketching over near the other side of the lobby as she stares at the front desk. I try to play off the fact that I'm staring at her, but it's too late; Nate follows my gaze and lets out a soft whistle, jabbing me in the side.

"What are you two wolves leering at?"

Nate continues to laugh as he turns to face Griffin Carlson, the hotel's chief of marketing.

"Oh, I see. Let me guess. That's the new decorator you were supposed to meet with this morning." Now both men are staring at Alison as I try to downplay the situation.

"Hey, Thor, what brings you down from the heavens to hang with us mere mortals?" Griffin smiles; since the day he was hired almost a decade ago, Nate and I have called Thor. It is an homage to his Norse heritage as well as his looming stature and striking blue eyes and blond hair.

He raises an eyebrow at me. "She's gorgeous. I hope you noticed."

"Oh, I noticed. I'm not blind. While I appreciate the ribbing, boys, you know she's not my type."

Nate shakes his head and shoves his hands in his pocket, letting me know he knows I am full of shit.

"Tell me, Vince...what about her 'isn't your type?'" he says with dramatic air quotes.

I roll my eyes and return my gaze to where Alison is still furiously taking notes.

"I won't deny that she's beautiful, Nate, but she's something else. She is one insanely uptight woman. You know I prefer them dumb and easy. Can't lie though; the thought of getting her to let that hair down and unbutton a few buttons is very tempting. Oh, and she keeps calling me Mr. Crawford."

"Ohhh, Mr. Crawford, is it? Should I be calling you Mr. Crawford these days, Vince?" Nate's loud laugh carries across the lobby, bouncing off the marble pillars.

"Very funny, Nate. Just keep on calling me the same old insulting names you usually do, alright? And let's not forget just how ridiculous you got when you found out Elise was into you."

Nate nods and slips an arm around my shoulders. "Something tells me you're going to be in a lot of trouble with this one. I can't wait to meet her. So why don't you go ahead and start introducing me before I do it myself and embarrass you?"

I know the bastard means it, too. Any chance Nate gets to make an ass out of me, he jumps at it.

"Gentlemen, if I'm not interrupting? Vincent, I need to speak with you about this year's internship program when you get a chance. If you could have your executive assistant reach out to mine to schedule something?" Griffin keeps his hands clasped firmly behind his back as he speaks to me.

"Yeah, of course, Grif." His jaw is set in a firm, clenched line. "Man, you gotta learn to relax. When was the last time you got laid?" Griffin's back stiffens a little, and he lets out a small exasperated sigh.

"On that note, gentlemen, I'll be on my way." He gives a curt nod and makes his way across the lobby.

"Come on. I can't have you making a fool of yourself in front of her. You'll have her running off screaming, and then I'll have to find someone who isn't half as good looking to get the job done to avoid a repeat performance." Nate says as we walk away from the column I've been leaning against and towards the grand piano at the far end of the lobby where Alison is set up for a moment.

"Excuse me, Miss?" Nate stops when he realizes that I haven't even told him her name before he marched over here to introduce himself.

"Ryder, it's Miss Ryder," I interrupt before she can reply. I see a look of annoyance flash across her face. I like that look; it means I am getting under her skin.

"Alison, let me introduce the CFO of Castille Hotels, Nate Baldwin. Nate, this is Alison Ryder, our new designer sent over by Madeline Dwyer Designs to whip our hotels into shape." The terse look on her face melts the moment she turns to greet him.

She holds out her hand to Nate, who promptly bows and plants a kiss on the back of it like a scene out of a Victorian romance novel. I can't help the eye roll that display earns. Nate's an absolute ham when it comes to women. He only has eyes for Elise, but he can't stop the comedian that comes out when he's around any woman, especially someone new.

"You'll have to forgive my best friend here, Alison. He has no idea how a beautiful woman is meant to be treated. He's far too used to the riffraff Hollywood types he spends all his time with." Nate grins over at me before returning his attention to Alison. "I, on the other hand, was not raised by savages."

He releases Alison's hand as he stands up, giving me a wink.

I am surprised when she laughs at Nate's little stunt. I haven't heard her laugh before. It is intoxicating, but a tinge of jealousy echoes through my body at the way she responds to him. Nate was right; this is going to be trouble.

"Well, I appreciate the gesture. It's a pleasure to meet you, Mr. Baldwin. I..."

Nate stops her in mid-sentence. "Nate. Call me Nate, and I'm going to insist you call him Vincent or Vince or anything but Mr. Crawford. You're going to have me looking over my shoulder for his grandfather to see what I'm in trouble for now."

She laughs again. What is it that Nate has in this whole situation that has escaped me? She's had her guard up against me since she walked into my office, but Nate has her laughing after a few sentences. I certainly never had an issue getting a woman's attention before, but this one is a firecracker.

"Alright, Nate." She emphasizes his name, seeming to struggle with the informality, but at least she is loosening up a little bit. Now to figure out how to get her to loosen up even more.

"You'll have to forgive Nate; ever since being diagnosed with a micropenis, he has to overcompensate with ridiculous behavior." I can't help but get a jab in at his expense.

She looks back over to me, her body instantly going stiff. I can't figure out if she hates me or what, but that shell is back up the instant her gaze meets mine.

"Well, he deserves a gold medal being best friends with you, Mr. Crawford, I'm sure you're better for having him around though."

"Oh, he's smarter than he looks, Alison, though I'm sure you'll figure that out sooner or later. Now if you'll both excuse me, I have some work I have to get done before lunch. Do make him show you the rooms upstairs himself." He smiles over at her again with that boyish grin. "There isn't a better tour guide in the building than Vincent. Look forward to seeing you again. Don't have too much fun."

I shake my head as Nate heads back to his office.

I turn back to Alison, giving her a smile. I'm determined to crack through that icy exterior.

"So, shall we?" I offer her my arm, which she stares at blankly. "I promise I don't bite…unless you're into that," I say a little lower, and I swear I see a soft blush creep up her neck.

This time, she takes my arm as we make our way to the elevators.

7

ALISON

This is turning into the longest day that I can remember. It is just now approaching lunchtime, and it feels like it has been ages since I walked into Vincent Crawford's office. It doesn't help that there is a war between the two halves of my brain regarding how I feel about him.

"So, the rooms we are going to see are vacant at the moment. I'll show you one of the standard rooms, an executive suite, and a presidential suite so you can see what you'll be working with." I nod once again, clutching my iPad tightly to my chest. I am hearing what he is saying, but my damn body is betraying me again. All I can think about is how perfectly he fills out his tailored suit. The way his eyes stare at me like they're burning a hole in my own. I squeeze my thighs together as the tip of his tongue darts out to lick his tempting lips.

His eyes catch mine, and I can tell he knows I've been staring at his mouth. *Shit! So much for subtly, Alison.*

"Actually, before we go on this tour, we should grab some lunch," he says reaching to push the lobby button to take us back down.

"No!" I half-shout in a panic while smacking his hand away from the button. "I—I have a busy schedule later, so I'd prefer to see everything now."

"I thought you were one hundred percent devoted to me during the duration of this contract," he says with a smile as he slips his hands in his pockets.

"I—uh yes, I am. I just forgot I had a previously scheduled thing tonight right after work, so I had planned on skipping lunch anyway." I could hear the stupidity in my excuse as the words tumbled from my mouth.

"Well, I'd hate to disrupt your schedule," he says with a laugh that tells me he isn't buying into my bullshit.

I'm usually great at turning myself off to focus on what I prioritize, but right now, that isn't working at all. I am having to do everything I can to keep my attention on taking notes about the rooms and not on noticing how masculine he smells or how his dark hair keeps falling over his forehead, or the way his long, thick fingers keep pressing against my lower back as we step into the first room.

"The only thing that we won't be changing are the beds. I hand-picked them to ensure the best quality sleep. Trust me; I tested out multiple options before making my decision. I'm nothing if not efficient when it comes to breaking a bed in," he says, throwing me an exaggerated wink.

And there it was…something that could have gone without saying, but it still makes me a laugh a little. His innuendos are anything but subtle or original. I'm not sure if that makes it pathetic or less aggressive, but it's a little funny, to say the least.

"Well, would you look at that: she can smile. I was starting to take it personally that only Nate got that pleasure."

The room is beautiful, with no luxury spared. There is no denying that this place was designed with opulence in mind. In most hotels, the rooms would have been better than average, but this is one of the premier luxury hotel chains in the world. They needed to be excellent in every possible way. The last time they'd been re-done was ten years ago when Vincent had originally purchased the property, and when they were completed, they must have been cutting edge.

Little things were starting to show here as well—wear on the furniture and carpets, fixtures that had lost their shine—and there was Mr. Crawford's vision of the hotel to take into account.

Chicago is known for its modern architecture: the clean lines and grid patterns that dominated the skyline, making everything sleek and geometric. Steel and brick are at every corner in this part of the city, and the buildings are tall and sweeping, making somebody feel as if they are in a man-made canyon when they walk down the street.

My brain is flooded with a million ideas, starting with the color palette. "While this place was designed with luxury in mind, the intensity of the deep reds and golds are a thing of the past. I see something entirely different for this renovation. Clean lines, muted colors, with an emphasis on black and white, allowing the structure of the building to be the shining star. It will bring to life that sleek, sexy, sophisticated idea you mentioned."

Keeping my eyes glued to the tablet or the features of the room kept them from taking in Vincent's structure instead.

I'm lost in thought as he rambles on. I can see a slight shadow of stubble that has started to develop on his jaw. The slight rasp in his otherwise deep, baritone voice.

At the moment, he's talking about the state the hotel had been in when he'd purchased it. He was only twenty-five at the time, a year younger than I am currently. I can't imagine getting together the resources to buy an entire building at this age. I am still only renting an apartment, not even capable or ready to purchase a condo, let alone a block-sized building.

"Come here." I turn around to see him sitting casually on the edge of the bed.

"Why? You look like a creep rubbing the mattress. Stop it." I can't help but smile as he strikes a ridiculous pose on the bed, trying to encourage me to come over.

"I just want you to experience the DreamCloud Luxury mattress. Trust me; this will make you never want to leave your bed."

I walk over slowly, turning around and sitting down on the mattress. He's right; it feels fantastic. It hugs my hips and cradles me, making me feel like I'm sitting on a cloud.

"It's nice," is all I can manage to squeak out. My mouth suddenly feels like the Sahara. Does he realize the effect he's having on me?

I look over at him; he's closer than I realized. My eyes drop nervously from his eyes to his mouth and back up again. Is it my imagination, or is he leaning in closer? I swallow hard and snap my attention back to the center of the room, ready to get back up.

"Lay back." He grabs my iPad from me and stands up before I can protest, pushing against my shoulder. I catch myself on my elbows before I fall completely back. "Just lay back for a minute. I promise, I won't tell anyone that I got you on your back the first day."

I don't hide my annoyance as I scramble off the bed and snatch back my tablet. "I'm going to use the restroom; I'll be right back."

I lock myself in the restroom and let my back rest against the door as I catch my breath. "Fuck! What the fuck!" I whisper as I turn on the cold water and stick my hands under it. I look at myself in the mirror. Gone is the perfectly polished Alison from this morning; now my eyes are hazy, my lips look full, and my skin is flushed. "Oh my god, I look turned on! Get a hold of yourself!" I say, dramatically pointing a finger at my reflection.

"Alison? Did you say something?" I can hear Vincent asking from outside the door.

"No, no sorry just—coughing. Felt a little parched is all," I say as I open the door and breeze past him.

"So, shall we head up to the top floor so I can take a look at the penthouse?"

The amused look on his face confuses me. That stupid smirk he keeps throwing at me is infuriating. It makes me feel insecure, like he's teasing me, but when he opens his mouth to reply, I can feel my cheeks heat up with embarrassment at my suggestion.

"Well, if you're that eager to head up into my apartment here, then by all means." He leans forward to press the button on the elevator, causing the hand he has against my back to drag a little too low for comfort.

I'm exasperated at the thought of being in his apartment, as well as at the feel of his fingers so close to my ass!

"But...I...we...it's not necessary, Mr. Crawford. Unless we're decorating your apartment, too?" I can feel myself blushing. I internally curse my fair skin for betraying me. Being alone with him in an assortment of random hotel rooms was difficult enough. Being alone with him in his apartment is going to be excruciating. As much as my brain is warring with itself, I know that even if presented an opportunity to pounce on him and rip his expensive suit off, I'd never act on it. He is right; I am uptight and rigid, something I am growing to hate about myself.

"No, I insist. I don't think it needs updating, but I could always use a professional opinion." He leads us into the elevators, scanning a key card at the reader before pushing the button for the penthouse floor.

"You'll have to excuse me for the security up here, but the doors do open directly into my living room. It wouldn't do to have guests pop in on me wearing my boxer shorts and watching a football game some random Sunday evening, now would it?" He laughs and glances over at me as we begin to move upwards one last time. I flash a small smile, acting as if I wasn't just picturing him half naked and sprawled across his couch.

"That would be unfortunate. I..." I am cut off by the doors opening into a huge apartment that takes up the entire top floor of the hotel. Everything is open, all the way to the windows that make up the wall. It looks out over the city with the most breathtaking view I've ever seen. The space is decorated immaculately, but that isn't what catches my attention. I walk straight over to the windows, my heels clicking against the marble floor. I'm marveling at the city beyond and completely forgetting whatever it was I was about to say.

"So, Alison, what do you think?" he says, walking up behind me as he slides his hands in his pockets. The deep tenor of his voice echoes in the open space. "It's the best view in the city, and it's all mine." I almost forgot where I was for a brief moment before he spoke.

"I have to admit, I'm jealous. My apartment overlooks a scenic alleyway from the fourth floor. My favorite part of the view is the stray cats fighting over the rat carcasses, but I'm also a little bit biased there since I grew up with a cat for a pet." I grin, hoping I convey the joke in the tone of my voice.

He doesn't respond. I look over at him and am once again overcome with another wave desire to kiss him. I bet he knows exactly how to handle a woman's body. How to make me fall apart and scream his name. He looks at me as if he has the same thought running through his brain. He takes a step closer to me as his eyes drop to my mouth.

"It's gorgeous," my breath hitches in my throat as I quickly turn my attention back toward the windows. I am certain I am not going to be able to look at him without doing something stupid. I can feel him moving behind me, and I can't take it any longer. I turn around to pull him to me, but he's walking away, towards the bar.

"What can I get you to drink?" He's removed his suit coat and tie and unbuttoned a few buttons on his shirt. I can see the tan skin of his neck and the small thatch of dark hair peeking out. I lick my lips, dragging my bottom one through my teeth as I picture myself slowly unbuttoning his shirt even further.

The sound of ice hitting the glass snaps me back to reality as he sets it on the counter in front of him. I glance up from the glass to his face and start to speak when he interrupts me.

"Don't tell me it's too early to drink again, Alison. It's after noon, and you made me work through lunch. Just loosen up and have a drink with me. I promise to be a gentleman. We've got a lot of work ahead of us, but we can afford to take a minute to relax and toast to all of the amazing work you're going to do for my hotel chain."

He reaches out and grabs another of the short glasses in front of him, dropping a pair of ice cubes in it and topping them off with the same whiskey he was drinking before passing it over to me. I take the glass, glancing down at it and back up to him before I agree.

"Alright, one drink. That's it, and then I need to get started on these sketches. I have some ideas for your hotel I'd like to capture while they're fresh in my mind."

"One drink isn't going to give you amnesia." He laughs and raises his glass, waiting for me to do the same. I raise mine to his before tipping it back and nearly choking on the burn of the strong liquid. I clear my throat, swallowing and coughing as I try to play off the fact that I might be dying.

"Maybe, maybe not. I'm a lightweight, Mr. Crawford," I say between coughs, looking back down at my glass as if it's going to help me out.

"Enough with the Mr. Crawford bullshit. In case you haven't noticed, I've been calling you Alison since you walked into my office back there. I think it's pretty safe for you to call me Vincent. I can promise you I'm not going to fire you for using my first name. In fact, I insist you don't call me Mr. Crawford again for the rest of the time we work together. You can call me Vincent, maybe bastard if the mood hits, but not Mr. Crawford."

He takes another long drag of the whiskey, chuckling as he sees the look of shock on my face. "The only time I allow a woman to call me Mr. Crawford is if she's on her kne—"

"Okay, Vincent, our meeting is concluded," I say, interrupting him before he finishes that statement. I take another long swallow of the whiskey, not noticing the burn as much this time now that my throat is already numb.

I walk closer to him and place the glass back on the bar as I meet his eye line. "I'll reserve the other names for after we know each other a little better."

Fuck, a little whiskey and I sound like I'm coming on to him. It half sounded like a pickup line, like I have plans to "get to know" him better in the future. A smile spreads across his face, and I can tell he's about to say something stupid. I throw up my hand to interrupt him.

"I only meant that I was going to be working with you for a long time to get all of these hotels done. Nothing more." *Shit, this whiskey has gone straight to my head. I could kick myself for blowing off his lunch offer earlier.*

He laughs outright, and I can feel the heat rise in my cheeks. It is the opposite of the reaction I was hoping for. The last thing I need is to encourage his behavior.

"Oh, I hope we do get to know each other better, Alison. I hope to prove I'm not half as bad as you think I am, or that I'm much worse. I'll leave that up to you to figure out." He refills his glass, adding a little more to mine before handing it over to me again. "So here's to a beautiful working relationship. Cheers."

"Here's to getting the job done right." I grab my glass again and lift it to him. It is the closest I am going to get to saying the word "relationship" regarding Vincent Crawford, and whatever happens, I am dedicated to making sure this gets done right, both for my sake and for the design firm. I owe Madeline that much for having faith in me. I just hope I can come out of all of this in one piece.

8

VINCENT

I watch Alison's delicate neck as she swallows the rest of the whiskey before she sets the tumbler back down on the bar.

"You don't need to be so in control, Alison. I promise I'm not trying to set you up for failure." I can see her shoulders drop.

"I'm sorry I've been...jumpy today. I'm not sure what's gotten into me but I thi—"

"It's because you're attracted to me." I watch as shock settles over her face.

"Excuse me?"

"I said, it's beca—"

"No, I heard you. That is *not* why!" Her face is bright red, and she places her hands firmly on her hips.

I set my glass on the bar top and reach for hers to do the same. "Alison," I say, stepping towards her. "I'm attracted to you. I have been since the second I laid eyes on you at the airport. You're stunning." I reach up and brush a small wisp of hair that has loosened from her bun. Her eyes, big and bright, look up at me as I tower over her.

"I—I..." She's scrambling for words as her eyes drop from mine to my lips. I reach out, slipping my hand behind her neck as I pull her lips to mine. They're soft and supple, with a hint of whiskey lingering.

Her arms stay rigid at her sides, but I don't relent. I place my other hand on the other side of her face, cradling her cheek as I begin to move my mouth over hers. Slowly, she starts to come undone. Her hands reach up against my chest and fist my shirt as our tongues dance together. A soft whimper escapes her as I lightly bite her lower lip before dragging my tongue across it, followed by another kiss. I suck her tongue back into my mouth, caressing it with my own, but as quickly as it started, she's pushing me back.

"No, no, this can't happen. I'm…I work for you. This is unprofessional." Her chest heaves with her words.

"It was just a kiss, Alison. We're two adults that are attracted to one another; there's nothing wrong with wanting to explore that." I place my finger under her chin and lift it. I lean down again, slower this time as I gauge her reaction.

She grabs the back of my neck, crashing my lips to hers as her firm tits press against my chest. I reach down and pull her skirt up to her waist, grabbing her thighs and lifting her until she wraps them around me, grabbing her ass in the process.

I back us against the bar as I deepen the kiss. I want to consume her, to own her. Our breathing is loud and labored as we both devour one another. I set her on the bar, reaching between her milky thighs to feel the wet triangle of lace at the apex. The sound of glasses clinking against each other snaps her back to reality.

"Oh my god. Oh my god." She buries her hands in her face as she pushes me away again. "This was a mistake. I can't do this."

She pulls her skirt down and straightens her shirt before reaching for her bag and iPad to leave.

"Alison, wait." She turns back to face me.

"I'm not asking for anything from you. I know you just got out of a relationship and I'm not exactly the kind of guy to offer one, but it's okay to enjoy each other, in whatever capacity that may be."

She gives me a curt nod before turning on her heel and leaving.

* * *

THE SUN IS SINKING below the horizon as I watch it from one of the chairs near the bank of windows on the west side of the apartment. This is one of my favorite places to sit at the end of the day, especially these summer nights when the sun sets at an hour I'm not in the office or attending a dinner.

But tonight, I am not paying attention to the colors that play across the sky. I am thinking about the events of the day, the way Alison jumped almost every time I approached her, the way her soft, pouty lips felt against mine. At one point, I ran my hand up her arm while I was kissing her, and she is the softest woman I've ever felt.

I think I'm starting to realize there is far more to my fascination with Alison than the novelty of her. It isn't just that she is beautiful. If I wanted a beautiful girl on my arm, I could have called one of a few dozen numbers in my phone. The truth is, I haven't stopped thinking about Alison since I met her weeks ago in Dallas. The attraction was instantly there, but the fascination, the obsession kept growing.

It also isn't that Alison is whip-smart either. I didn't get this far in life by surrounding myself with stupid people, even if I joke with Nate about the women I tend to date; I pride myself on being able to see potential in people. One of the first things I did once I established my business was to create an internship program for bright, young minds. I wanted to nurture that in the younger generations.

After Alison had left, I did my research, as far back as I could find. I found out who her father was, learning that he owns his own law firm back in the small city she'd grown up in and that her mother is president of the local junior league. Her younger sister is a student at the University of Chicago, the same school that Alison and their father had attended. Both girls were legacies of the school. It would have been easy to think that she was nothing more than a girl who'd had her way in life paved for her before she even started.

However, she'd been top of her class, graduating with a 4.0 in dual degrees of art and interior design. She'd earned a full scholarship, based on merit alone. It was impressive, even on paper. In person, I immediately knew it was earned. She might not have come from the same background I did, but she had worked her way to where she was, whether her family had been there as a safety net for her or not.

I am shaken out of my thoughts by the sound of my phone ringing. I glance at the screen, laughing to myself when I see my best friend's name pop up on the caller ID. I need a friendly ear to talk out what is running through my mind before I get so lost in my thoughts, I run off to go surfing in South Africa. I pick up the phone without a second thought and don't wait for a greeting to start the conversation.

"Alright, buddy. I know you've been waiting all day to take a shot at me about this morning. I'm surprised you didn't call before now."

I can hear the loud, clear laugh on the other end of the line. His laugh is unapologetic; it brings back memories of the two of us growing up together, doing all the stupid things that teenage boys do between the times we were buried in books and getting ready for college entrance exams.

"I decided you needed time to get through with Alison and then process whatever the hell seems to be going on in your head right now. And before you say a word, yes, I noticed—the entire lobby noticed. And don't say it's just her looks because you were staring at her something fierce, man. I can't blame you there. She's gorgeous, but she's a pistol. You're going to have your hands full, and I'm going to enjoy watching every minute of it I can." I drag my hand over my face in exasperation before speaking again.

"Fuck me, man. She is...something else. I'm ninety-nine percent sure she hates me with every fiber of her being."

Nate laughs even harder now. I would be laughing at Nate if he were in the same boat; he was in the same boat just over two years ago, actually. Back when he'd met Elise, she'd hated him and for good reason. In fact, she despised him so much she made it her vendetta to see that man suffer. I'm pretty sure she would have castrated him if she could have gotten away with it. Now, I couldn't imagine him with anyone else.

A brief wave of embarrassment washes over me as I picture what I must have looked like today, following her around the lobby like a puppy. I'm completely screwed.

"I hope you enjoy watching me get shot down because I'm pretty sure she thinks I'm about the most disgusting man on the face of the planet."

"Nah, she's just not used to your particular brand of charm yet, bro. I'm sure you'll convince her like you do every other woman."

"Did you see the way she looked at me? It was like I was something vile stuck on the bottom of her shoe. Besides, she's got a job to do. I should leave her alone and let her focus. And we both know I'm not looking for anything serious; she just happens to tickle my fancy at the moment." I drum my fingers on the wooden arm of the chair, debating if I should tell him about the events that transpired just a few hours earlier.

"Right, and that's why you've canceled all your appointments next week to go with her to New York? You can try to convince yourself you wanted to go out there and go skydiving or whatever else it is you're telling everyone you're skipping out to do, but you're not going to be able to convince me that you have any motives other than being out there with Alison."

I begin to reply, but I can't lie to Nate, even if I am trying to lie to myself; he knows me too well. I take a deep breath, letting it out in a long exhale without saying a word. In the end, I decide not to tell him about the kiss. Something insides me feels like it would be betraying her trust and I don't want anyone else meddling in things.

"Yeah, that's what I thought. Go on and tell everyone else whatever it is you need to but be honest with yourself. It's good to see someone who makes you try. I was getting tired of models and actresses who don't know how to spell Chicago, much less find it on a map." The amusement in his voice would be irritating if he weren't right.

A small chuckle escapes my lips. "Well, I think we both know she won't have a problem with your litmus test. That being said, I'm pretty sure she can manage well enough in just about any situation. However, if being able to spell the name of the city where we live is your only requirement, then you overshot the mark with Elise. She's vastly smarter than you!"

"Yeah, well, I'm pretty sure Elise is smarter than all of us put together. That's why I snatched her up. I figured out she was the whole package and decided I didn't want anyone else to get ahold of her before I could. Maybe you could take some lessons on that front."

"Ha! Might I remind you that Elise proposed to you because you were dragging ass!" That is one story I'll never let him forget or live down. He is lucky he found a determined woman who loved him that much.

"Yeah, yeah, well, I already had the ring, so potato, potato. Even if Alison thinks you're a useless and an arrogant asshole, at least you know she's not interested in you for your money, right?"

I rub my fingers across my eyes, letting out a soft groan. "I mean, she's not particularly interested in me at all other than as an employer, and I ought to keep it that way, but fuck me, she is one helluva woman."

"Keep telling yourself that. I'll remind you what you said later, when the time comes. See you tomorrow." The other end of the line goes dead, and I turn my attention back to the skyline.

The sun has sunk below the horizon, and the lights of the city are flickering to life. I love this view but my mind is a little torn tonight. In a few days' time, she and I are set to fly out on the company jet to New York, the first of several locations we are going to together.

I keep telling myself that it is going to be strictly business. I simply want to oversee the progress at each of the hotels and make sure that Alison has whatever she needs to get her work done. I am going to let her get to business without too much interruption, but if an opportunity arises to get to know her better, I won't miss it for the world. Then again…maybe she wants a strong, confident man to give her some direction.

That thought immediately has me rigid in my suit pants. I move to adjust my rock-hard cock. I let my head fall back and imagine her on her knees in front of me.

"Mr. Crawford, is there anything I can do to please you?" I can hear the words tumbling from her full red lips. That pink tip of her tongue darting out to wet them before she wraps them around the head of my dick.

I groan and open my eyes, downing the last of my drink before feeling like a sick piece of shit for objectifying her like that.

9

ALISON

I have been completely lost in the job for several weeks now, spending almost every minute I have in the office drafting up drawings and combing through fabric samples and furniture catalogs to find exactly what I'm looking for. After my last encounter, I've been avoiding him like the plague. I'm still in shock that it happened, that I know how he tastes, how his body feels pressed against my own. I snap out of my thoughts before I get lost in a long daydream like I keep doing.

Now that I'm settled in at my new place, I feel better, at home at least. Work is spent dodging Vincent at the hotel. I'm often running from room to room and back to the lobby to check on the renovations while Vincent pops in to make sure I have what I need.

My office back at Madeline Dwyer Design is full of samples, and so is the bag I carry home each night, but I've found almost everything I was looking for. I need to get as much done as possible before I fly out to New York with Vincent.

At least that is what I am telling myself. I am highly motivated to knock this project out of the park. It is, after all, my chance to not only impress Madeline and cement my place at the firm, but it is also an opportunity to impress Vincent. Having a recommendation from someone like him would grant me carte blanche in this industry. This job is huge. It is going to take every ounce of creativity and concentration to make sure that things go smoothly, and the designs are flawless. Madeline always reminds her designers not to let personal vision overpower what the client wants, but she also reminds us that we were the trained professional and it is okay to let a client know what worked and what didn't. We are like a personal guide through design land, helping to get the client from their vision to the end goal.

I grab my phone off the table, checking my messages again. I shot a text off to Janelle an hour ago about being out of my mind, but she still hasn't replied. That isn't much of a surprise. It's a Friday night, and Janelle is probably out doing something a lot more fun than stewing in her dorm room.

Janelle is a knockout, always the social butterfly and life of the party and never one to pass up a good time. She loves everything about life—at least everything that makes her feel like she is alive. Unlike me, she doesn't feel like she has anything to prove. She's changed her major three times before settling into the English program with a marketing minor, and even now, no one is quite certain that is where she is going to end up. Janelle keeps saying that she just wants to experience everything that life has to offer before she settles.

It is the sound of banging on the door that takes my concentration from my work and brings it back to the world around me. I didn't even realize it was dark out. The last time I looked outside, the sun was just setting, casting a beautiful pink and orange haze through the room.

I push up from my desk and go to the door. "Who the hell?" I say pulling the door open cautiously. There is Janelle with a bottle of wine in one hand and a bag full of Chinese takeout in the other. I shouldn't be surprised.

"So, you said you felt like you were going crazy. I figured you needed something to take the edge off, and I can't think of anything better than red wine and MSG to wind down after a hard week.

Besides, you're leaving for New York tomorrow, and this is my last chance to see you for a while."

She leans against the wall, blonde hair pulled into a ponytail and feet clad in a pair of black sneakers, nearly bouncing on the balls of her feet when she moves to come into the apartment.

"I feel like I haven't seen you in forever, Ali; what gives? That job sucking you dry yet?"

I smile and move to one side to let my sister in; this girl always knows how to make a situation better. I ought to have known the radio silence meant Janelle was up to something. Last time I sent her a text about being sad because my boyfriend forgot my birthday, she went radio silent, then showed up dressed in a full clown costume and face paint, making balloon animals.

"Something like that. You know you didn't have to come over here like this. I know it's Friday night and you're still young...but I'm so glad you did. If I stare at that computer for another minute, I'm probably going to go insane." I flop down into one of the dining room chairs and rest my forehead in my hands.

"I'm also a little stressed about this trip tomorrow. I have no idea how I'm going to spend a week with Vincent Crawford without going crazy either. This is going to be a long week."

Janelle is cracking open the bottle of wine while I complain. She fills two glasses almost to the rim before taking a long swig straight from the bottle. I promptly take two large gulps before diving into the bag of takeout.

"Well, first of all, *you* are also young. Just because I'm younger than you doesn't mean you're an old lady yet so get that shit out of your head." Janelle points at me with her glass before raising it to her lips and taking a long drink.

"If you keep up that stupid attitude, next thing you know, I'm going to find you in a nightgown surrounded by fifteen cats. You seriously need to stop thinking that being responsible and having fun are mutually exclusive. Live a little, Ali; it's sad how much time you spend buried in your work." I take another drink as she walks over to the table and rubs my arm. I know she's right, but it's hard to change.

"I know, I know. It's just...ugh. I'm at such a pivotal point in my career, Elle; I need to prove to Madeline and Vincent that they can trust me on this job. It's just hard when he's so god damn infuriating!"

"Is he that bad? What's he been doing?" She takes a big bite of her eggroll and looks at me intently.

I take another gulp, finishing off the wine in my glass, uncertain of how much to tell her. The two of us are best friends; we have been since we were kids. Janelle is only three years younger than me, and we were inseparable until I left for college.

There was a reason that Janelle had come to join me in Chicago when it was her turn to go to college, too, and it wasn't because our father was an alumnus. Janelle has been the one who'd talked me through every last one of the relationships that ended in the past ten years, from my first boyfriend back in sophomore year of high school through my most recent dumpster fire of a failed engagement. She also knows my tells well enough to know when I am trying to hide something.

I glance at the floor as I watch her pause, put the glass down, and look me over with a long sigh. I can tell I don't need to say anything else.

"Dear God in heaven, he tried to sleep with you, didn't he?"

"What? No!" I lie. "Yes, okay, maybe a little; we kissed. We made out. He had my legs wrapped around his waist and his massive, hard cock pressed again me, okay!" Janelle is laughing while clapping her hands in excitement. "But seriously...the way he kissed me. It would make a sinner blush."

"So, what's the issue? You struggling to remove your judgment about him from the situation? Or you worried it won't fit?" she says with a stupid grin on her face.

I groan and put my head down on the table, unable to look her in the eye. She knew before I even opened my mouth, so there was no point in denying it. I am not ready to audibly admit that I am attracted to the man...or that I can't seem to control my body's reaction around him, or that I want nothing more than to have him rip my clothes off, spank me, and make me call him daddy.

"Yes, but he's a total playboy, Elle; god knows how many women he's been with or where his dick has been last. Also, WILDLY UNPROFESSIONAL!" I shout, waving my arms around erratically. I lay my head back down on the table like it will help make my problems disappear.

"So, what you're telling me is that you're getting paid good money to go on an around-the-world trip with a hotter-than-hell billionaire to do the job that you love—a billionaire who specifically stalked you, found your firm because he clearly wants you, and thinks your clearly capable of taking on this massive job—and all you can say is he's a total jerk? Oh, and he's got a huge dick and knows how to kiss you into next week." She laughs and grabs a fork, prying open one of the containers she'd brought with her and stabbing a piece of the chicken that lay on top. "You are some kind of stupid, sis."

I take a long breath and chance a glance up at her from over my folded arms, nodding a little. I am unable to come up with a good explanation for why I am the way I am.

"Janelle, I cannot just go prancing around the world like I'm some fucking princess on vacation with her billionaire man. This is my career and reputation that I have worked so hard for. I cannot fall for this emotionally unavailable and complete cliché of a playboy!"

The amused look on Elle's face is maddening. She is barely fighting off another laugh. "I'm serious, Elle. There's nothing fun about any of this. I'm in crises mode here. Clearly, you don't know me that well," I huff, grabbing the wine bottle and filling my up my glass again.

"Oh, I know you pretty damn well, Ali. I know you're not going to do anything fun if it means setting a single toe out of line or doing anything less than what's expected of you. I just think you're insane for not just having the time of your life while you go traipsing around the world on Vincent Crawford's dime. And I'd have a hard time keeping my hands to myself if that one was willing. I'm just saying is all. You need to let loose and have a good time for once in your life. I'm not saying sleep with the dude if it makes you that uncomfortable;

just have a good time for once! Where is always following the rules going to get you?"

That grin on her face is so typical of her. Janelle lives for a good time. She would enjoy this a lot more than me. I envy her.

"Well, I'm hoping it's going to get me into a promotion and a nice job at the firm so I can move into a nicer apartment for starters." I stab at the food in front of me with a huff.

"Oh my god. Like you're not going to do a good job, Alison. You're better than everyone at that firm and Madeline knows it. If she doesn't, then she's an idiot. The fact that she put you on this account says it all. She didn't have to say yes to Vincent Crawford. You need to give yourself some credit. And please, stop acting like you have to be the saint because I'm the sinner of the family."

I shake my head. "Yeah, well, the best way to convince her that I'm not as good as she thinks is sleeping with a client."

"Sleeping with a client?" I can hear the faked shock in Janelle's voice. "Why, whatever do you mean, Miss Ryder? I was just suggesting that you might make the best of your upcoming trip and enjoy the sights that each city has to offer."

"Save it. I know exactly what you meant. You'd be in so much trouble if you were me, and you know it."

"Seriously though, Ali, I'm not saying sleep with the guy. I get that's a conflict of interest and unprofessional or whatever. I'm just saying loosen up, go on an adventure with him if he invites you, and try not to act so uptight around him…like you always are. You can be friendly with your clients; it's ok. I promise you won't catch cooties."

"He did…" I focus on eating the food in front of me, not sure I want to admit what I'm about to say to her.

"He did what?"

"He kind of offered like a friends-with-benefits or no-strings-attached type thing." Janelle's face turns completely serious as she leans across the table and grabs both my hands.

"What exactly did he say? I can't believe you almost didn't tell me this!"

63

"He said something about how he doesn't do relationships and that we could just enjoy each other in whatever capacity that may be."

She throws her hands in the hair, tossing mine up along with hers. "Oookaaay, screw what I just said; you need to bang the shit outa that man! Seriously, Ali, you are not going to get an offer like this again. I mean...wow. Silver platter," she says as she holds her hand out as if there were a tray and points to it. She fans herself dramatically.

I snort at her comment and almost choke on my food. Raising my hands above my head as I cough and laugh at the same time. I put my head on the table again, trying to recover.

"Don't die on me, Alison. Just promise me one thing," Janelle says as she leans down, brushing a stray hair behind my ear.

"What's that?" I clean my chin with the napkin and grab some water.

"Consider his offer. Don't over think it; just go with what feels right, and if being intimate with him doesn't feel right, don't do it." I smile at her sweet sentiment.

"I do, however, hope you get the chance to choke on his *huge* co—" I jump up before Janelle can finish her statement.

"Stop teasing me about him!" Janelle jumps up from the table and runs as I chase her into the next room.

VINCENT

New York has always been one of my favorite hotels to visit. It doesn't hurt that the Long Island Skydiving Center is just a quick trip away from the hotel. It has been too long since I've jumped out of a plane. I've been itching to since deciding I was going to be accompanying Alison on this trip.

I pull up outside Alison's apartment, about to step out of the car when I see the door to her building open and her bustling out.

"Let me help you," I say as I jog up the sidewalk to grab her bag.

"Thanks, you're a little late." I can't help but smile at her extreme attention to detail.

"You know, your type-A psycho behaviors are really starting to grow on me," I say with a wink before turning the car on and letting the engine roar to life.

"This car is so impractical; you could have told me we'd be in a convertablllllle!" She draws the last word out as we launch into traffic.

When I decided to drive my 1968 Aston Martin convertible, I knew I'd catch shit from her, but I love this car.

It's a quick drive to the airport, and since we're taking my private plane and aren't leaving the country, it's a relatively quick and painless process. Once boarded, it's just a two-hour flight, during which I plan to try my hardest to get her to agree to join me in skydiving once we reach New York.

"So how do you feel about heights?" I ask as we settle into our seats. At least I can pretend it is under the pretense of making sure she isn't scared of flying at first. The question doesn't throw her too much off guard as she glances out the window.

"Not too bad. I mean, I've flown plenty of times before." I laugh, reaching for a bottle of water the flight attendant hands me.

"Well, I was asking because I'm planning on going skydiving on Long Island while we're in the city, and I was hoping you'd join me." I try to act entirely nonchalant as I raise my bottle of water at my suggestion, but the look of horror on her face tells me it is going to be a flat-out no.

"I...I..." She is stuttering, stumbling over her answer.

"Relax, Alison; it's not like I asked you to pilot the plane." I reach over and place my hand on her arm, immediately regretting it. The warmth of her bare skin makes my mind instantly wonder what it would be like to feel other parts of her warm, soft body. Images of our bodies tangled together as my tongue explored hers come rushing back to me.

"I was just hoping that you'd come skydiving with me. You're free to say no, but I think you'd have an amazing time. Long Island is only an hour and change away, so once we land, we could zip over and board another plane." I take another sip of water, keeping my focus on her face as I wait for her reply.

"Umm..." She fidgets with her fingers and shakes her head. "I'm sorry, Mr. Crawford, I mean Vincent." I can see her cursing herself internally as she speaks. "I'm not a fan of falling out of planes on purpose."

By now, the plane is taxiing out onto the runway, and the pilot is making his announcements and preparing for take-off.

"I mean, I don't plan on falling out of this one, but with the proper equipment, falling can be fun, Alison. Trust me: I'd never offer you anything but the best."

"I'll pass. Thank you." She glances back out the window, ignoring

66

me as the plane moves to take off. Silence falls between the two of us, but I can see her grip on the armrests as we ascend. She is a little more bothered by heights than she cares to admit.

"If you won't come skydiving with me, at least join me for dinner." Her eyes get that wide look again, like I've just asked her to jump out of this particular plane right now without a parachute. I am not sure how to take that. I just asked her out for dinner, not out for a night of wrangling poisonous snakes. She's still on edge since our make-out session.

She clears her throat, opening the bottle in front of her and taking a sip of water. She looks back out the window before answering me.

"While I appreciate all the offers, Vincent, I'd prefer just to order room service tonight and settle in. I have several emails and things I need to go over for the Chicago location still. I do appreciate at the offer though."

"Is this because of what happened between us? Alison, I don't want you worried that every time I invite you to do something I'm just trying to get in your pants."

"You mean you're not trying to get in my pants, Mr. Crawford?" Her comment takes me aback. A sly smile spreads across her face, and for the first time in my life, I think I feel a slight blush creeping up mine.

"Well, since you ask, yes, Miss Ryder." I lean forward in my seat, resting one elbow on my knee as I reach my hand up to touch her chin. "I am trying to get in your pants. In fact, I can think of little else besides imaging how sweet it will be when you finally surrender yourself to me and allow me to sink into your tight, wet core."

Her tongue darts out to wet her lips as her throat bobs with a hard swallow. I can see she's nervous, but I'm not done. I want her to know without question what I want to do to her.

"I want you panting, begging me for release." I reach up and rub her earlobe between my thumb and forefinger, causing her eyes to flutter. "I want to hear my name on these lips." I move my hand from her to drag my thumb across her lower lip. "And just when you think I'm done, when you feel like your body can't possibly handle any more pleasure, I'm going to bring you over the edge, over and over again." I lean in just a tad further and ever so softly press my lips to hers before pulling away quickly and settling back in my seat.

"Did that answer your question?" I look over at her to see that she still hasn't moved.

"Mmmhmm."

The rest of the flight is uneventful, almost silent. She focuses on the drawings on her tablet, making sure that she has everything in line for back in Chicago before she starts things in New York. I catch up on my email and current events the rest of the flight. As much as I want to, I decide against idle small talk in favor of giving her space. I want those words to simmer in her head.

After we land, I usher Alison to the car I had scheduled to take her to the hotel while I make my way to catch the next train to Long Island. That's how I find myself, sitting in a tiny passenger plane, wearing a bunch of gear, while the instructor pulls the door open.

I don't have to go through all of the basic training since I've been jumping for years now. They just let me rent the equipment and run through a quick reminder on safety procedures before we boarded the plane with a few first-timers. The others are new to this; most of them are tandem jumping with an instructor to make sure that everything goes well.

I am waiting to go last; I want to enjoy every last second of this jump. God knows I need the stress relief and mental distraction. There is a lot going on, between the renovations and the purchase I am planning to make soon in Vancouver. It is always stressful buying property in another country, especially when it is an already established hotel. Previous owners tend to be persnickety about their property.

And then there is Alison. Usually, I wouldn't care what anyone else thought of me. My grandmother had always told me it was none of my business what anyone thought about me. I've taken that lesson to heart.

There is something about her, though. Some part of me secretly wants to impress her, but there is more to it than that. It isn't just about impressing her. I want to make her let go of all those things she is holding onto so tightly.

It is my turn to jump anyway, and all my focus goes to getting ready to jump from the plane and the impending free fall. I always enjoy that moment of anticipation. That is the moment in which my heart is pumping while I watch the ground below, looking like a patchwork quilt of land, trees, and buildings that stretch on for miles. One breath and I let go, just falling into the air as the world rushes up to meet me.

This is letting go, letting all the worries melt away as I fall into the air. This is what I needed, and what Alison needed too: to just let go. Maybe it is up to me to help her realize what she is missing.

11

ALISON

The driver pulls up to the hotel. I step out of the car and take in the impressive exterior of the building as he gathers my bags. This is my first time in New York City. Chicago is large, I am used to that, but there is something about the pace of life in New York that no one is prepared for until they experience it.

My mind is still a complete jumble from the flight. It took everything I had not to jump into his lap and drag him to bedroom on the jet. I've never had a man speak to me that way, to be so bold, so brazen about what exactly he wants to do with my body. It was refreshing, exciting to know that a man so powerful wanted me and wasn't afraid or ashamed to express it so thoroughly.

"Alison?" I hear my name in an unfamiliar voice. Vincent told me on the flight that someone would be waiting for me when I arrived at the hotel to make sure I got settled and to show me around the place. It has been a long day, and I am ready to get situated before I start on the next part of the job.

I turn to see a tall, slender woman walking through the revolving front door of the high-rise, dressed in a business suit with carefully styled dark brown hair that matches her eyes perfectly. I hold out my hand out to greet the other woman with a handshake as she approaches.

"Yes, I'm Alison, but you'll have to forgive me, your name is completely slipping my mind at the moment. It's been a long...week." I smile apologetically.

"Oh, not a problem. I completely understand working with Vincent," she says with a bit of an exasperated smile. "Vince can be exhausting when he's got a beautiful woman in front of him." She laughs and directs one of the doormen to take my suitcase into the hotel as she guides us into the lobby.

"I'm Elise Taylor. You met my fiancé, Nate, back in Chicago. I'm Vincent's attorney. Normally, I'd be in Chicago myself, but I had some business to take care of here in New York. It's a pleasure to meet you. Nate had nothing but good things to say about you and the work that you've already started back at home. I'm kind of excited to see what kind of new life you can breathe into some of these properties. God knows it's past due, and Vince is about as good at decorating as I am at water skiing."

I immediately find myself warming to Elise; she is beautiful, accomplished, and clearly doesn't take shit from Vincent. I'll have to ask her for some pointers on that front.

"It's so nice to meet you, Elise. Nate is wonderful and seems to keep Vincent in check. He made me feel very welcome back in Chicago."

Elise steps away for a moment, grabbing a key card from behind the reception desk, saying something to the hotel manager before walking back over to where I stand.

"Well, that's good to hear. Nate can be such a ham, so I'm glad he didn't make you feel uncomfortable. Come on, I'm sure you're tired from traveling, and there's time to start work later. You can get a nice overview of the hotel on our way up to your room. I think you should change and then come down here and join me for a few drinks in the hotel bar."

I open my mouth to protest. I want to get started as soon as possible on the work I am here to do. I convinced myself it would all just be easier if I focus on nothing but work.

"But, I…"

"No buts. I insist, and drinks are on me. I don't get a lot of other women to keep me company around here. I'm usually just subjected to spending all my free time around Nate and Vince. Please do me a favor and let me entertain you for the night. The work will wait until tomorrow."

Elise is convincing enough that I give up trying to fight and just go along with her. A drink sounds like a great idea actually, and much needed now that my sexual frustration is at Chernobyl level.

"Alright. I think I could use a night of relaxing anyway; I've been working for weeks on the Chicago site without a break." The doorman comes by with my suitcase.

"Good. Now, the porter here can show you to your room. Get comfortable and come meet me back here in the lobby when you're ready."

It doesn't take me long to head upstairs and grab a quick shower, changing out of the business clothes I'd worn for the flight with Vincent and into some nice jeans, a blouse, and strappy heels. Janelle made me pack them just in case I needed something casual for the time I was here, and I am so glad she did.

I step off of the elevator and make my way to the lobby bar, glancing around until I see Elise waving me over. She already has two glasses of wine waiting for us; I like the way this woman thinks.

"Come on. I made them pour us both a glass of Vince's best wine and charge it to his account." She laughs as I settle into the chair opposite her. "Don't look so mortified. He can afford it. Next round is on me, I promise."

I sip from the wine, stifling a little laugh. "I mean, I don't doubt that. I just don't want him to think I'm getting paid to sit around here and drink his wine."

"Alison, you're fine. Trust me. I've known him, and Nate, for years now. Neither of them is going to hold it against you if you take a little time for yourself. Didn't Vincent go running off to go skydiving? He's a big work hard, play harder kind of guy. Now relax a little and have a good time. It's Saturday evening. We're in New York City. You're young and gorgeous. Just enjoy it."

"That is exactly what my sister would say to me right now." I take another sip of my wine and smile at Elise. "You remind me a lot of her."

"I'm sure she's a beautiful and intelligent young woman then," Elise says, laughing with a dramatic flip of her hair.

"Well, yes, that, but also she's not afraid to live in the moment and actually enjoy it. I, on the other hand, struggle with letting loose."

"Well, we will have to work on that then. And don't worry about Vincent. I'm sure he's making you uncomfortable. You're going to have to excuse him for being such a little boy sometimes. He really can't help it; neither can Nate. Those two grew up together, and I don't think they forgot what it was like to be teenagers. Besides, it keeps them out of bigger trouble," she says with a slight wink.

I laugh, feeling myself relax a little more. "So, what you're telling me is I'm working for the world's richest little boy?"

"You could say that. I'm sure all of his ex-girlfriends would agree." She toys with the rim of the wine glass in front of her. "But I don't think any of them ever knew him very well. They were all just fascinated with the money and the life. When the novelty of it all wore off, they were gone before the dust could settle on reality. Vince really does have terrible taste in women."

"Sorry, I guess I don't know him either. We've only just really met recently. We actually met before at the airport in Dallas; it was random and wasn't my best performance." My voice trails off as Elise grabs the bottle of wine the waiter left on the table and refills both our glasses.

"Oh, I don't know about all that. He's gone on about you to Nate a few times now." Elise laughs again and looks over me. "I dare say you've made a better impression than you thought. Besides, I've seen photos of what's going on back in Chicago. You know what you're doing. That much is clear. I've got high hopes for the rest of the sites. And as far as Vincent goes, well, he puts up a front for most of the world, but at heart, he's still the same little boy who was growing up on his grandparent's farm back in the middle of nowhere. If I know better, it was Vince that didn't make the good impression. Sometimes he lets the thrill of the chase get the better of him. In all honesty, he's harmless. If he's pestering you or crossing a line, just tell him and he'll back off."

Elise's words aren't exactly what I had expected to hear. There wasn't a ton of information about what Vincent's life had been like before he'd become a hotelier.

"I, uh...he's just infuriating!" I let the word slip out, unsure of what I actually wanted to say. Elise laughs heartily like she knows firsthand what I am talking about.

"You know, years ago, I went on a blind date with Vincent. That's how we officially met. Actually, I had gone to college with him, so he looked familiar when I walked into the date, but I couldn't place him." My mouth drops open.

"What?" She laughs at my shocked response.

"My college roommate Tara worked for his non-profit, and she set us up. I had just moved back to Chicago from DC, and I was temporarily living with her again. It wasn't love at first sight by any stretch of the imagination. There was just zero chemistry between us; I was put off by his...bravado," she says with a small laugh. "He did invite me to come interview with him because he was in need of new legal counsel and I was jobless, so it worked out perfectly. Long story short, I knew Nate from college, and when I interviewed at the hotel, I saw him, and we ended up reconnecting, and, well, now we're engaged."

"That is crazy! What a small world. You mentioned a farm? That's a surprise. I wouldn't have pegged him for a farm boy."

"Oh yeah, both of them. Nate's father worked for Vince's grandfather when they were back in school. They've been friends ever since. It was a long way from mucking out horse stalls to owning hotels all over the world, so I can't blame you for being surprised. He doesn't exactly give off that corn-fed country boy air." Elise is a talker, but I am thoroughly enjoying it. She is friendly and funny, and I hope that the two of us can be friends. It doesn't hurt that Elise is feeding me information on the topic I find most fascinating right now.

"Not at all. I mean…if you go by what you read about Vincent online, then you'd be pretty certain he was born with a silver spoon in his mouth and didn't have anything better to do with his life than chase leggy models around a penthouse apartment." I kick myself for going too far with that one, but the wine has me feeling a little too relaxed.

Elise grins. "Appearances are deceiving sometimes."

I nod in agreement. "I can't deny that. I guess if you went by what I look like, you'd think I was just a pretty face or another 'dumb blonde.' I have fought against that stereotype most of my life."

"Then you ought to know that there's usually a lot more to a person than what meets the eye. Yeah, he drives an expensive car, and he has a penchant for dating beautiful women and doing things that put his life in danger to pass a Saturday afternoon. But, he's a lot more than that. You don't see the news stories about the charities he started. How he's sending a half dozen kids from his hometown to college because their parents can't afford it, or how he's made a point of hiring veterans at all of our locations because his grandfather was in the Army once upon a time. He dates models, but he also funds a women's shelter in every city that he owns a hotel. The journalists don't think that stories about a billionaire giving back or making a difference with the less fortunate are what sells papers. Maybe they're right. Just know that what you read on the internet isn't the whole picture."

Elise put everything into perspective. She hit a dozen points that I hadn't considered. Most of them were things I didn't even think to ask or consider when it came to him. I figured I'd known everything I needed to know about Vincent when I'd walked into his office on that first day, but maybe I was wrong about him. Maybe I need to give him another chance.

12

VINCENT

The last few days have flown by. I had hoped to spend more time with Alison, but she was like a damn tornado tearing through this place. If she wasn't buried in designs and contracts, she was on her phone or sketching on her iPad. The few times I had interacted with her, she seemed distracted but weirdly nicer. Kind of freaked me out.

"Alison?" my voice rings out in the executive suite, but there is no sign of her. I walk through the rooms that make up the suite, admiring all of the changes. I pick up a scrap of material and let it slip through my fingers when a sound behind me alerts me to her presence.

"Shit!" she yelps as she trips over a ladder that was left out in the walk-in closet. She was too buried in her iPad to notice and stubbed her bare toe. She had removed her heels and cardigan and pulled her long hair up in a haphazard bun.

I take a moment to admire her in the few seconds before she notices me. Her exposed neck is long and slender, just begging for me to drag my lips against it.

She is startled to see me when she emerges from the closet, and her face displays her surprise. "Oh, hi! I wasn't expecting anyone this late." She quickly tries to regain her composure and smooth out her hair, realizing she is barefoot and in a slinky camisole.

I make no effort to avert my eyes; in fact, I make an extra effort to take in this moment...Alison with her guard down. Looking terribly mussed up and sexy. Long strips of her hair hang down her neck from her bun, and one of her spaghetti straps drapes off her shoulder. I am lost in my thoughts when the sound of her clearing her throat brings me back.

"Well, Elise told me I could find you here and that despite all her best efforts, she couldn't get you to leave or even stop for a bite to eat."

Alison scurries around me, grabbing her cardigan and shoes. "Well, since I'm only here for a short time, I need to get everything situated and running smoothly. I still have so much to do and so little time, so I need to make sure everyone sticks to the timeline, and we stay on schedule."

"I certainly appreciate all the work, you are a machine, but you really should get something to eat. Care to join me tonight?" I nervously run my fingers through my hair, waiting for her reply. I can't remember the last time a woman made me nervous.

She continues to scurry around the suite, gathering scraps of material and blueprints. "I appreciate the offer honestly, but I'm exhausted and just want to get some room service and finish up some paperwork in my room."

I can sense her tenseness and decided not to push her tonight. I am captivated by her work ethic and passion; it permeates every aspect of her actions.

"Well, in that case, I do hope you follow through on that plan to get some food and relax. I'm sure we'll catch up tomorrow, so I'll leave you to finish up your evening. Oh, and Alison, remember that you can always fly back to the hotel locations we are visiting as the projects progress. That's what the plan has always been." I turn and walk out of the suite, the entire time wanting to pull her hair out of that messy bun and throw her down on the king-sized bed in the middle of the room.

I make my way back to my room but then decide to head over to the onsite restaurant instead. Usually, I'd be out at one of the finest restaurants in the city, then hitting up my favorite club. I don't know what has gotten into me lately, but the truth is I am getting bored of that lifestyle. It is empty and exhausting.

"Hey, Frank, how's it going tonight?" I shake the hand of the maître d'.

"Good evening, sir, very busy tonight but we have your regular table if you'd like?" He gestures to a secluded booth in the back of the restaurant.

"Not tonight, Frank. I'll sit at the bar. Probably going to be a liquid dinner tonight, buddy." I give him a pat on the shoulder as he lets out a hearty laugh.

I put in my order for a medium rare filet and sip on the whiskey my bartender sits in front of me. I reach up and loosen my tie, letting out a long, exasperated sigh. I feel like I've been holding my breath and didn't even realize it. I reach into my pocket and pull out my phone to call Nate.

"Hey, old man, you manage to scare off Alison yet?" His laugh echoes on the other end.

"Yeah, something like that. I promise I'll be sending Elise home to you soon."

"Yeah, I talked with her earlier today; she said she's been spending time with Alison. Apparently, they hit it off. But seriously, how are things going?"

I rub my hand roughly over my five o'clock shadow. "I can't stop thinking about her, man. I have tried to get her to go to dinner or just a drink, even sky diving. She fucking hates me."

"Listen, you're approaching this all wrong. First of all, you're technically her boss, so she probably doesn't want to cross a line. You need to cultivate a friendship and then, when the contract is over, maybe it can turn into something more. You need to come at it from her point of view, try to find out what she's in to, and see if you can get in the door that way."

"Ah, shit, you've been hanging with Elise too much. You are way into your feelings, bro." I down the rest of my drink and motion to the bartender for another.

"You're just pissed that you've finally met a woman who you can't just fuck into wanting you or doing whatever you want. Just don't be a dick to her, Vincent. Hey, Elise is calling. I'm going to let you go. Let me know how it goes."

I hang up the phone and promptly down the entire second glass of whiskey. I know Nate is right, not just because it's the respectable thing to do but because Alison deserves better. I pick at my steak, but I've lost my appetite. Instead, I opt to drown my sorrows in an endless glass of liquor.

It's nearing eleven when I finally pry myself away from the bar. I can feel the room start to spin as I make my way to the nearest elevator bank. I stare at the buttons as the doors close and then re-open again. I press the button for my floor and lean back against the wall as I ride the car up to the twentieth floor.

I'm walking down the hall to my room when the urge to knock on Alison's door overtakes me. Her room is right next to mine. When I had my secretary book the rooms, I specifically asked for side by side placement. I don't know what I was thinking; maybe that she'd be more apt to sleep with me if we shared a wall.

I find myself standing at her door, willing myself to walk away. I bring my hand up to knock when my phone vibrates in my pocket. I pull it out and see a familiar name on the screen. Vanessa.

"Hello?" I answer, a bit confused. I haven't spoken to Vanessa for at least six months. She was a casual fling I would call when I was in New York. We both had separate lives and had zero expectations when it came to things between us.

"Hey, handsome. I heard you were in town and you didn't call me," she says with a fake, syrupy sweetness. I can tell she's pretend pouting.

"Sorry, sweetheart, just been a very busy few days."

I step away from Alison's door and head into my room.

"So, are you going to make me ask?"

"Ask what, Vanessa?"

"Are you alone?"

I lean against my door and close my eyes, letting the line go silent.

"Hello? Vincent?"

"Room 2017. There will be a key waiting for you at the front desk," I say and then hang up, throwing the phone on the nearby couch.

13

ALISON

I finish up gathering my things and head to my room. I am still mulling over Vincent's comments about revisiting the hotel sites...it made perfect sense; I was just surprised I hadn't considered that option yet. I had been killing myself to get everything done on the first trip. This past week had been beyond exhausting. Surprisingly, Vincent had given me plenty of space to get the ball rolling here in New York, but the days were certainly not without a comment or two from him or a dinner invitation.

I flop on my bed and let out a loud sigh. I haven't spoken to Janelle this entire trip, so I pull my phone off the nightstand and send her a quick text.

You awake?

My phone rings immediately, causing a smile to break out on my face.

"How did I know you'd still be awake?" I laugh into the phone as Janelle launches into what she had been up to the past week.

"How's the New York trip going?"

"Good. I have been able to get so much done, and my vision has meshed well with Vincent's, so that's a huge relief. There have been a couple hiccups. Oh my god, I ordered the—"

Janelle interrupts, "What I really mean is how are things going with the sexpot billionaire? You do anything crazy yet? Had two drinks at dinner? Get matching tattoos? Cut out of work at four-thirty?"

I roll my eyes at Elle's sarcastic remarks. I should have known she was just fishing for info on Vincent.

"No, nothing crazy, unfortunately. I have been working round the clock, but I'm hopeful it will set everyone up for success once I leave. I have spent some time with Elise Taylor; she's the company attorney, and I think you would love her. She reminds me a lot of you actually. She's kind of taken me under her wing so that I'm not completely alone and going crazy through all of this."

We chat for a while longer before I turn in for the night. I only have one more full day in New York before I head back to Chicago to wrap up things there and then head off to Denver.

I am just about to fall asleep when I hear mumbled laughing and talking in the room next door. I distinctly make out a deep voice talking followed by higher-pitched laughing...the banter continues for a while but quickly turns into moans and what I can only assume is the headboard slamming against the wall.

"Are you fucking kidding me?" I mutter to myself as I pull a pillow over my head and groan. I consider banging against the wall, but just as I pull my arm back to send a message to the moaning offenders, I realize that my room shares a wall with Vincent's.

"Why the hell am I not surprised? All of my judgments confirmed." I huff loudly and roll over, pulling the blankets over my head. I can't deny I am angry...angry for starting to let my guard down and think he could change.

I can't sleep. I whip the blankets off of myself and head to the bathroom. I turn on the shower and step in, letting the hot water cascade over my body. I can feel the tension melting from my neck and shoulders. I take my time, allowing myself to relax and giving the chance for the spank-fest next door to die down.

After a good forty-five minutes in the shower, I dry myself off and lather myself with lavender lotion and oil to help myself relax. The cool sheets feel so good on my clean body, and it seems like the situation next door has finally stopped.

I have just nodded off again when a ping from my phone alerts me to an incoming message. I roll over, groaning to myself as I reach for the phone on my nightstand. I jolt up immediately as I read the name that registered on the screen: *Vincent Crawford.*

My stomach flip-flops as I swipe across the screen, revealing the message.

Hey...you up?

* * *

THE NEXT MORNING, I do everything in my power to avoid Vincent. So far, I've been successful, spending my time immersed in finishing up a few projects and meeting with vendors.

Things have been going very smoothly so far, and I plan to keep it that way. I have just one more meeting before I need to finish packing and head to the airport. Our flight is leaving tonight, and thankfully, Vincent has some off-sight meetings to attend to this afternoon, so I am confident my plan to avoid him will work.

The sun is just beginning to set. I look out over the city from my room. I do love it here; maybe someday I could open a firm here. I stand for one more minute, taking in the beautiful yellow-orange light that filters through the room. I grab my bags, give the room one quick glance to make sure I have everything, then make my way toward the elevators.

I had told Elise I would meet her at a quarter to eight and we would take a car to the airport. I am just emerging from the elevator when Elise and Vincent both wave me over to where they are standing. I want to slap the shit-eating grin off of Vincent's face but decide not to let my frustration show.

"You ready to get out of dodge?" Vincent asks, taking my bags.

I give a tight smile and turn my focus to Elise, giving her a quick hug. "Ready to get home? I bet Nate's missing you like crazy."

"Well, I'm certainly ready to get home. I can't lie. I'm worried about the state of our apartment. That man is a genius in the board-room, but it's like he's allergic to cleaning. And to be honest, poor Griffin is probably so tired of having to babysit him. God knows when I'm out of town, he always tries to get Griffin out of his comfort zone. I don't know why these boys can't leave that poor man alone." We both laugh and make our way toward the sidewalk as our car pulls up.

"Griffin is only a few years older than Nate and Vince, but they tease him so much. He's a little more tightly wound and reserved, so they're always making a game out of trying to get him to lighten up."

"It's all in good fun; Thor knows that. Besides, we'd hate to see him live his entire life so uptight and miss out on some fun and life-changing experiences," Vincent chimes in.

I ignore his comments that are so clearly directed towards me.

"Maybe I can set my sister up with him," I joke. "God knows that girl needs a leash sometimes." I shake my head as Elise chuckles and rubs my arm sympathetically.

The commute isn't exactly quick or easy since this is New York City, but I am thankful Elise is there to keep me company and keep me from having to engage Vincent one on one or strangle him. We finally board Vincent's private plan and are about to taxi when Elise hops up to use the restroom, leaving Vincent and me alone in the cabin.

"You look like you have made an unimaginable amount of progress in the short time we have been here. I know we discussed a lot of the preliminary plans, but seeing it brought to life is just amazing. You are a fantastic designer, Alison; I hope you know that. I can't wait to see how all of this turns out."

I smile, smoothing out my dress. I can't miss my chance to be snide. "Thank you, it has certainly been exciting and challenging at the same time. I honestly think the re-branding and updating of your hotels is a worthy investment and you'll see a big return on it." I turn to pull my laptop out of my bag before adding, "The only suggestion I would have for you is to consider soundproofing your rooms. It's amazing what you can hear through the walls."

He is listening intently when suddenly his face goes white and his back stiffens. Maybe he doesn't even remember last night, which is why he hasn't brought it up. Whatever is going through his head, it certainly isn't something he wants to relive or remember. I bite back a smile at his discomfort, glad I can make him uncomfortable for once.

He opens his mouth to speak when Elise comes back from the restroom and settles into her seat. "Okay, what'd I miss?" she says with a cheeky smile that quickly fades when she senses the tension that has settled over the cabin.

I smile over at her and grab her hand, launching into a discussion about her wedding plans and upcoming nuptials. I am not about to drag Elise into any issues I have with Vincent, and I also am not interested in his apologies or excuses. The fact is he owes me no explanations for his behavior, and I have no right to care…now if I could get my brain to understand and believe that.

VINCENT

Two weeks have passed since Alison and I went to New York to start renovations at the hotel there, and things seem to have changed between the two of us…dramatically.

Even the sight of me seems to piss her off more than usual. We spent a week there while she toured the rooms, came up with ideas, and explored the furniture and fabric that was available in the city. I know she heard me with Vanessa, but nothing happened. As soon as I gave her my room number, I texted her back and told her not to come, but she did anyway. She tried forcing herself on me and my drunk ass ended up knocking over a desk and chair trying to avoid her.

Elise had found a fast friend in Alison, and the two of them had been practically inseparable during their time together. I could barely get a word in edgewise when the three of us had to interact or spend any amount of time working together.

Then there was that week with nothing. After our flight home, Alison had dove into her work; I hadn't seen or heard from her in days. It wasn't until I called her to arrange the flight to the hotel in Denver that I heard her voice. I knew she'd been buried in work because the staff in New York was getting instructions and diagrams about the new decor that were quickly being put into place, but she hadn't responded to any of my correspondence directly. She had sent over plenty of designs, invoices, and contracts that I needed to sign but nothing in the way of actual conversation, and everything went to my executive assistant. I even noticed a few Mr. Crawfords in the emails; good to know we're back to that.

Maybe that shouldn't bother me, but it does a little. I enjoy seeing her name in my inbox or on my calendar. I look down at my phone every time it vibrates, hoping to see her name across the screen.

I'm not going to pick her up this time for our flight. She'd said she had her ride to the airport and would meet me at plane. I'd been waiting for about fifteen minutes when she arrived.

"About time, Alison." I glance up from my watch with a sly grin. "I was starting to believe you were going to skip out on me."

Alison lets her suitcase rest beside her as she shrugs. "Trust me; the thought crossed my mind. But in the end, I decided there's no way I was missing out on an all-expenses-paid trip to Denver. I've never been there before. So what death-defying feat are you planning for Colorado? Any chance it will be something that will keep you out of my hair and sight for the entire trip?"

She is joking with me, which seems to be a good sign, at least a little, even if there is some underhandedness. That has to be a first.

"Skiing." I smile broadly as she raises an eyebrow in my direction. "From a helicopter."

"Oh, I should have known." She grabs the handle of her suitcase and heads towards the small gate where our private plane is boarding. "Come on; we have a flight to make."

I follow her down the ramp onto the plane, letting the attendant stash our bags in the proper compartment on the plane. There is something different with her; she is being way more engaging than she ever has been. Something is up.

"So, I know better than to ask you to come skiing with me, but are you going to join me for dinner this time? There won't be any Elise there to entertain you." I kick myself for asking, but I am a glutton for punishment as far as Alison is concerned.

"Before you say no! Let me please apologize for my behavior in New York. I should have been more...thoughtful about where your room was located, and I'm embarrassed, to be honest. If it makes it any better, I was drunk and no—"

Alison puts her hand up to stop me.

"You don't owe me an apology; it's none of my business what you do in your spare time, and honestly, I shouldn't have been surprised."

Her words sting a little because it is the truth. She did see me as just a man-whoring playboy...I guess I proved that to her in New York. I sat there staring at her without saying a word. I don't know what to say to make things right, so I figure keeping my mouth shut is the best option.

After several awkward minutes of silence, Alison lets out a long sigh. "Alright, Vincent. Dinner tonight, but I have to get to work tomorrow. After all, you're not paying me to hang out with you. You couldn't afford me, anyway. Oh, and in the future, don't booty-call your interior designer after you bang your latest conquest...not good for morale," she says with her newfound sarcasm.

I have to fight hard to keep the surprise off my face when she agrees, but a huge smile spreads across my face seeing her stand up for herself and tell me off.

"As I said, there wasn't any banging."

"Don't worry about it; it is in the past. Clean slate and all that, right?" She gives me a coy wink and snaps her seatbelt on.

A huge grin spreads across my face at her attempt to make light of the situation as I move to buckle myself into my favorite seat on the plane. I want to ask more about the booty-call comment because that bad decision isn't rushing back to me. However, she said yes to dinner, which means I have some planning to do. My phone is already in my hand, sending out emails and texts to all the appropriate parties to make sure things are in motion.

"Fair enough. Dinner tonight. I'll meet you downstairs in the hotel at eight, if that's alright with you?" I raise an eyebrow, waiting for her reply.

"See you at eight," she says without looking up from her phone. She giggles as she reads what looks to be a text.

"Ma'am, please put that in airplane mode," I joke, trying to keep the fun mood going.

She finishes typing and hits send before turning the phone off and turning to me. "Sorry, just had to let my boyfriend know I'm taking off."

15

ALISON

I have no idea what came over me…why the hell did I just lie to him about having a boyfriend? The truth is I had been texting Janelle to let her know I was taking off and that I'd text again when I landed. I panicked after I agreed to go to dinner with him: another stupid move on my part. I curse myself internally…and Elise. This is all her fault!

Elise and I had gotten to know each other even better since we'd gotten back from New York. Elise had even gone out with Janelle and me for a girls' night out. As I predicted, Janelle adored her, and the two of them clicked immediately. They have a lot in common. They both have the philosophy that life was meant to be enjoyed, so why not grab each opportunity and live life to the max.

Since I'd been home from New York, I'd been in a mood and Janelle had let me know at every opportunity. I hadn't wanted to admit it, but she was right…is it the fact that I am jealous Vincent had been hanging out with another woman? Or is it the fact I'd purposely sequestered myself from him? I'd never admit this to anyone, but he had entered my mind several times over the last few weeks…mostly at night when I was trying to fall asleep. Thoughts of his hands making their way up my trembling thighs, of his lips against my neck and my breasts.

So, I shouldn't have been surprised when Elise had brought up Vincent on the way to the airport this morning. There had to have been a motive for her to offer me a ride to the airport. She lived only a few blocks down from Vincent, so her suggestion that it was easier for her to give me a ride over him made no sense. It was just as much out of her way as it was out of his, and she didn't even have any business at the airport for an excuse.

She had clearly wanted to talk about how he was a nice guy, and how I ought to give him a chance, even after I told her about the headboard banging against my hotel room wall. Elise knew him far better than I, but in the time I'd been around him, I still hadn't seen this amazing person she described. She told me to try to look past the brazen comments and somewhat reckless behavior. Even after all his frustrating behavior, Elise's comments were sinking in. Maybe my subconscious wants to give him another chance, and that's why I agreed to dinner. Maybe I am judging him the way I felt people had judged me in the past.

The fact is, he's kind to everyone who works for him. There isn't a moment when he's treated any of them like just employees or ordered anyone around. He notices them, which is more than can be said for a lot of billionaires. He consistently praises me for my work, noticing even the smallest of details. He even called Madeline to tell her personally how great of a job I was doing.

Elise had told me about Vincent's charities and the things he poured his money and time into. There is more to him than just extreme sports and fast cars and women. There is a depth to him that I hadn't thought was there, and for some reason, he is interested in my success: a poor, just barely out of college woman, ten years younger than him, who turned her nose up at him. All of that had been swirling around in my head when Vincent asked me to join him for dinner again. He'd asked me before, back in New York, but I'd turned him down. This time, I wasn't able to hold out.

The part of me that doesn't want to keep him out is getting stronger every day that I spend with him while the part that is resistant grows quieter and quieter. I am growing more confident by the day…it is all just a fun time and I certainly don't have to explain my actions to anyone! Maybe Janelle was right when she said that I am too uptight for my own good. Vincent isn't the marrying type, so why not take a carefree approach and live in the moment? I'm young and beautiful; I could have a good time without worrying about the long term, right?

But now, we're in Denver. We check into our rooms in the hotel: matching suites on one of the upper floors. He is right next door, only one wall away, and my heart is pounding in my chest in anticipation of what is going to happen tonight. Will I be able to keep my newfound confidence, or will I wilt under pressure and end up giving him a piece of my mind?

I rummage through my suitcase. All the clothes I've brought for the trip aren't what I want to wear. They are all either far too casual or far too much about business for a dinner out. I didn't plan for this, and now I am starting to freak out. Grabbing my phone, I shoot off a quick text message to my sister.

For some dumb reason, I agreed to go out to dinner with him, and now I have nothing to wear.

I toss the phone onto the bed and go back to comparing two outfits that are never really going to make me happy when my phone goes off. I grab it and glance at the screen to see a reply from Elle.

Look in your closet.

My brow knits together. I walk over to the double doors on the other side of the bed. I hadn't even bothered to open them when I'd arrived, but just behind them is a red cocktail dress that is exactly my size and a matching pair of high heels resting on the floor underneath them.

What have you done? I wanted something better than I brought, but this screams sex on a stick!

I tap out a reply to her before pulling the hanger down, admiring the dress. It is going to fit like a glove.

It wasn't me. It was Elise.

I can't decide if I want to hit or hug Elle and Elise for doing this, or how they'd known I was going to say yes this time. In the end, it doesn't matter. I agreed to this dinner, and I am going to look like a million bucks when I walk into it. The dress and heels are fabulous, but I am nervous that it might be a little too much for dinner with my pseudo-boss. Now, I need to get ready and get my nervous sweating under control. I walk over to the minibar and grab the vodka. "Nothing a little liquid courage can't fix."

A couple of hours later, when the knock at my door comes, I am startled. Vincent agreed to meet me in the lobby, so I wasn't expecting anyone. Thankfully I am ready. My blonde hair is in loose curls down my back. I opted for winged eyeliner and lots of mascara, just a touch of shimmer on my lids, bronzer on my cheeks, and a nude lip to give the look a sultry but not overdone vibe.

I open the door gingerly and am met by a smiling Vincent. I am not certain what to make of the expression on his face, but I am glad I overdressed for the occasion. I don't even want to know how much his suit cost, but I'm confident it would cover at least a few months of rent. He looks like he was made to wear it too, filling it out in all the right places. God, why does he have to look so damn good all the damn time?

"Well, good evening, Alison." He grins. I can see a glint in his eyes as he looks me up and down. He's looked me up and down before, but this time, something is different. He looks like a man that hasn't eaten for a week and just sat down in front of a thirty-two-ounce steak. I take in a breath and pull my bottom lip between my teeth, being careful not to mess up my lipstick.

"Good evening, yourself. You look nice." I smile at him and take his arm he offers me. His cologne is intoxicating; mixed with his own scent, it immediately sends my brain spinning.

"I think you stole my line, but you look more than nice. You're stunning." He leads me down the hall towards the elevator, but I become confused when he pushes the button that calls the elevator to take us up.

"Up?" I glance at him, and he returns my questioning expression with a grin.

"You'll see, but yes, we're going up."

We stand quietly together as we wait for the elevator. My arm is still looped through his, and I can feel my body begin to sweat nervously. When the doors open onto the roof, what I see drags a little gasp from my parted lips.

"Oh wow…Vincent, you didn't have to do any of this. I mean, none of my other clients have ever made this kind of effort!" I am taken aback by the set up on the roof. Lights have been strung around a single table set with a white tablecloth, attended by one of the hotel's wait staff. The view from the top of the hotel is breathtaking; the Rocky Mountains surround us, still sprinkled with snow on the peaks. It is clear he's done this so we could be the only two people in the world for at least a little while.

"Well, I know I didn't have to. I just wanted to." He laughs softly and takes my arm that had slipped free when we stepped off the elevator. He leads us over to the table where the waiter pulls a chair out for me to sink into. He moves to the opposite side of the table to join me and signals for the waiter to get our drinks. He returns with a bottle of wine, filling our glasses before bowing slightly and disappearing through the doorway near the covered area where the elevator was located.

"I mean," I look around the roof with a soft laugh and then back to him before continuing, "what is all this? You buttering me up for something? Is there another hotel that I need to redecorate unexpectedly? Or are we jumping off the roof?" I point towards the ledge with a sly grin on my face.

"No, no unexpected hotel additions, Alison, or death-defying activities. It's simply a date."

He is entirely relaxed as he drinks from the wine glass in front of him. I am stunned for the moment, and I know the fact that I am speechless shows on my face because he takes the opportunity to speak again.

"I mean, I don't do this sort of thing for every woman who works for me, Alison. I know you think I'm free and loose with my time, but I promise, I don't do this for just anyone. In fact, I don't think I've done this ever before."

I don't know how to respond, so I take a long drink of the wine in front of me. I am trying to process what is going on, but I am not sure I am going to be able to wrap my head around the fact that I am sitting across the table from one of the richest men in the world, having drinks on what most people would have called our first date. Part of me wants to put an end to this immediately, but my sister's words ring out in my head to just relax and take it for what it is.

"I guess I'm wondering…" I look up at Vincent, fingers still wrapped around the stem of the wine glass. "Why do it for me then? I guess my sister was right when she told me I hadn't been on a date in so long that I wouldn't know one if it bit me on the ass."

What am I saying? I haven't had enough wine to blame it on the alcohol. I also haven't had enough to feel as brave as I do at that moment, eyes locking with Vincent's across the table, but he doesn't look away. He keeps my gaze in his, even when the waiter appears with two dishes in hand.

"Oh, I think she underestimates you, then." The waiter puts the plates down without a word, removing the silver-colored domes to reveal a plate of pasta: chicken Alfredo, my absolute favorite food. I am not sure I want to know how he knew what I like, but I have a feeling that I have Elise to thank or blame for all of this. I'm pretty sure that the topic of favorite dishes came up at some point in one of our conversations.

"I'm pretty sure both of us might have been underestimated here, Vincent." I pick up a fork and stab it into the food on the plate, swirling it around to gather the noodles as I glance back up at Vincent. A grin is on his face as I let out a groan of satisfaction.

Elle and Elise are probably back at home just waiting to find out how tonight goes. I don't know because I left my phone back in the hotel room, but they both had a hand in this. I am not sure whether I want to yell at them or hug them both.

"You may be right there. I feel like we got off on the wrong foot, and god knows my behavior in New York certainly didn't put any of your thoughts about me to rest." Vincent smiles at me; it is warm and genuine. I can tell from the way that it traveled through his features all the way up to his eyes.

"One of the few things I'm good at is knowing is when I'm wrong, Vincent." I try to soften my expression. I had been wrong, especially about him. I am not convinced in the slightest, though, that this man is anything more than a good time. A mere distraction on my road to a true happily ever after.

"Oh, I bet you're good at a lot more than that." His voice is matter of fact, and he keeps his attention on me rather than the plate in front of him as he eats. I glance away nervously; I'm not a fan of being the center of attention. Maybe I have a touch of social anxiety.

It is one of the reasons I haven't even thought about dating since my breakup with Brian. It has only been a few months anyway, and work is providing a much-needed distraction. Frankly, I don't have the time to try to fit another person into my life right now.

I feel the heat rise in my cheeks when I process the compliment. I am not sure whether he meant anything more by it or not, but I know exactly where my mind went. Hopefully, the light up here is low enough that he isn't going to notice my flooding with color.

"I guess I'll have to leave that up to you to decide since I'm the one who's working for you." I grin up at him. A very loud and large part of me knows that mixing business with pleasure is entirely wrong, and an even bigger, louder part of me wants it more than anything else right now.

"Right now, you're off the clock. This is entirely pleasure. I promise." He stands up, leaving the food forgotten on the plate that he's barely touched and offers me his hand.

"May I have the pleasure of a dance, Miss Ryder?"

"But there isn't any music." I look around the roof. We are alone, not another soul there, and I can't figure out if he planned this and there is some secret source of music that is going to surprise me any moment or if he's lost his mind.

"And who says we have to have music to dance?" He grins down at me. With that smile, I can't resist. I take his hand he's extended and stand up from the table. There isn't much point in fighting any of this anymore. I am here. Maybe it is time to give up and enjoy myself for once in my life.

I let him slide one arm around my waist and pull me into his arms as we begin swaying back and forth. All of a sudden, I don't know why I've been fighting all this time, but the rational part of my brain isn't exactly working at the moment. The part of me that had been urging me to let go all of this time is feeling pretty vindicated though. This is everything that has flowed through my daydreams since I met Vincent. I keep telling myself it's just a date. Nothing serious, and nothing to freak out over. Just go with it!

His firm body feels amazing pressed against mine. I can feel my nipples harden against his chest. I want so badly to be taken by him. I run my arm up his, pausing for a brief second to feel the strong bulge of his bicep.

My brain is still battling with itself when he leans in and presses a soft kiss to my lips. I tense at the unexpected intrusion as he tightens his arms around me, deepening the kiss into something that steals my breath and leaves me feeling a little dizzy.

My lips don't move, and my body stays rigid, but all too quickly, I give up on resisting. Moving my hands from his shoulders up to his neck, to run through his dark hair and lose myself in the way it feels to be held in his arms. His tongue darts out and slips past my lips, massaging my tongue with his own as his lips caress mine. I can taste the sweetness of the wine on his tongue as he continues to explore my mouth. I am drunk on this moment, a moan involuntarily escaping my lips against his. I can feel him growing firm against my belly; I want to touch him, to feel his manhood pulse in my hand and inside of me.

I am not ready when he pulls away, but it is only then that I realize how much my lungs are screaming for air. I take in a gentle breath and the chance to glance up at him nervously, not sure what to expect. His eyes are heavy and full of lust.

"So, is this how you treat all the hired help, or I'm just lucky?"

He lets out a loud, unguarded laugh. It is nice to see him relaxed as well, not focused on trying to run a company...just living in the moment.

"No, Alison. I'm the lucky one. I seriously doubt you go around dancing with and kissing all your clients, so I'm going to take being the exception to your rules as flattery."

He's right. This is against all my rules. It is the first time I've stepped out of the boundaries I set for myself, and it is turning out to be one of the best decisions.

"You should. All of this is a first for me. I don't make a habit of dancing without music; it really sets the mood, ya know." I bite my bottom lip, trying my hardest to flirt...something I am not exactly a pro at. Tonight, I am going to be selfish, and maybe a little bit reckless for the first time in my life. It would make Janelle proud.

The whole thing is brought to a jarring halt when Vincent opens his mouth though.

"I like the soft moan that you let out when I kiss you," he says, leaning in to run his nose and lips up my neck, stopping only to nip at my jaw.

Thoughts of hearing moans through the walls of his New York hotel flood back to me. How could I be so stupid as to think he was suddenly different? How could I be so stupid as to think I could have a casual and careless fling with someone who was banging his way through the entire Victoria Secret roster?

"I can't...I..." I step back, breaking his touch.

"You can't what, Alison? What is it?"

"It's New York. I know you made it clear from the beginning you can't offer a relationship and it would be purely casual, but I'm not like that. I can't be with someone who's sleeping with someone else right after kissing me." I turn to leave, but he grabs my hand.

"Alison, wait, please. It wasn't like that. She came up to my room, but nothing happened. I knew it was a mistake and I tried sending her away, but she came on to me. What you heard was me moaning because I fell over a desk and knocked over a chair. I swear nothing happened." He's clinging to my wrist tightly.

"But you invited her up to your room, didn't you? Even if you didn't go through with it, you wanted to long enough to invite her over. Casual or not, at the end of the day, I don't want to be someone's flavor of the week." I pull my hand free, leaving him standing there with a look of complete shame and disappointment on his face as I step into the elevator and the doors close.

I wring my hands as I ride the elevator back to my floor. Do I even care if he thought about being with another woman? Why can't I just use him like he would me? I let out an exasperated groan and stomp down the hall to my suite. I know the answer...I know I'm falling for him, and this cannot end well.

When I get back to my room, I draw a bath, filled with essential oils, to wash away this frustration. A warm soak always helps me decompress and calm my nerves. I strip out of the dress and pick up my phone to text Janelle but decide against it and set it on the counter.

Grabbing wine from the mini bar, I pour myself a glass before lowering into the water and closing my eyes...I just need to simmer for a bit and ignore the question of why I can't seem to fucking relax and stop trying to control everything.

I sink back into the warm, aromatic water, inhaling deeply. "God, I've needed this," I mumble, letting my head hang back against the edge of the tub. It is deep and jetted, something I plan to keep as part of the new design of the hotel.

I let my mind wander to the events that unfurled earlier...I have to admit, I may have overreacted a little, but his comment was a complete mood killer. Had I just been looking for an excuse to bail like I always did?

I roll my head around, trying to relax as one of my hands squeezes a sudsy loofah against my neck. I replay the kiss in my head...the way his lips pressed against my own. His tongue had darted out and caressed my own as his firm body pressed against mine. Before I can stop myself, my hands are skimming down my breasts, settling between my legs.

My breathing quickens as I begin to rub my clit. My eyes flutter as I imagine Vincent's long, thick fingers touching me. My movements become more erratic as my pulse races; I couldn't stop now if I wanted to. It isn't long before I'm squeezing my legs together, thoughts of Vincent Crawford's tongue lapping at me like a man starved for my taste.

"Fuck!"

I slap the water as I shoot up in frustration; it's ok, it's fine...I'm fine, I tell myself as I come down from the explosive orgasm that just rattled my body.

16

VINCENT

I kicked myself as soon as the words left my mouth. One thing I need to learn is that Alison is vastly different from the women I previously charmed.

The other women in my life were easy to get and easy to lose, something I had prided myself on in the past. I want to be different for Alison. I know she deserves so much more. I had called after her, but she bolted anyway.

I don't know what came over me; it felt like jealousy. I'd felt it bubble up in my chest when she first mentioned having a boyfriend on the flight out here. It had been sitting in my stomach, stewing.

A feeling of possessiveness gripped me so tight when I held her. She's mine. The thought of another man touching her, holding her, kissing her, made me sick to my stomach. It also made me act out like a fucking child. I have to make things right. I am not just going to walk away this time.

I make my way back to my room to clear my head and give her some space. I pace the floor with my phone in my hand, finger hovering over the call button. Finally, I give in and hit send.

"Hello?" Elise's voice echoes on the other end.

"Listen...I fucked up. Majorly."

* * *

I KNOCK SOFTLY on Alison's door. Waiting hopefully.

She opens it slowly to see a remorseful looking me standing there with my hands in my pockets and my head hung low. I am hopeful my body language conveys just how sorry I am.

"Alison...I feel like you're going to tire of this song and dance very soon, but I want to extend my apologies once again for my behavior. Before you say anything, just hear me out, please." I look down the hall and then motion past her. "May I come in?"

She looks down at her robe-clad body and pulls it closer against her chest. I'm becoming very aware of her nakedness under the plush covering.

"Umm, yeah, yeah just let me..." She seems unsure of what she is saying. She ushers in me and stands at the end of her bed. She seems nervous, fidgeting with the belt on the robe.

I sit on the edge of the small couch and place my elbows on my knees. "I won't stay long, but I need to apologize. I know this isn't a valid excuse, and it's a flimsy one at best, but the past...women I've engaged with have been very different from you. They...how do I say this? They were after one thing and needed something from me. You're completely different from anyone I've ever pursued or engaged with, and I am asking for your patience and forgiveness."

She stands silently for the longest time, probably trying to process what I am saying or maybe to determine the best way to tell me to fuck off. She hugs the lapels of her robe even tighter to her chest before she finally speaks.

"Thank you; I do understand what you're saying. I am not great at letting my guard down, in case you haven't noticed, so when I do, and things go south, my gut instinct is to put up a wall. I felt great coming here, and when you brought up the moaning comment, it just made me think of New York, and I realize I'm no different from the random woman you hooked up with there, and I get that. I guess I just didn't like being reminded that I'm just another notch in some random guy's belt."

I lower my head when Alison brings up New York. "I know. I knew as soon as the words left my mouth that those memories were probably where your mind went. She was someone I used to date a while back. She heard that I was in town and reached out. I know it wasn't right; I regret it now. I was frustrated that I couldn't seem to get through to you, and I took her up on her offer for a drink. I knew her intentions, and I should have said no, but I didn't." I rub my thumb and forefinger across my brow as I speak.

"Look, Vincent, you don't owe me an explanation for your choices. We have a professional relationship and how you choose to spend your time or who you choose to spend it with is none of my business. Honestly, it's fine. I'm just glad we realize now that we should keep things professional. I shouldn't have kissed you back tonight; I work for you."

I am not sure if she is trying to convince me or herself. "And you have a boyfriend...which is whole other apology I owe you. I was completely out of li—"

"Actually...I made that up." She looks down at her feet as confusion washes over me.

"Wait, what?"

"I—I'm sorry. I don't know what came over me when I said that on the flight. I was texting my sister. I think I just hoped if I said that, you would back off on the flirty comments. I was confused; you're my client, and I can't risk my job for some meaningless hookup that could destroy my reputation. I thought I could let loose and live in the moment without feelings. I was wrong."

I sigh and run my hands through my hair. I can see she isn't going to change her mind tonight. "I understand. I really am sorry, Alison; I hope I haven't damaged our working relationship. I would like to be friendly with you...hell, I'd like to actually be friends with you, if that's possible." I stand up and shove my hands in my pockets, looking at her with a questioning eyebrow raise.

She lets out a small laugh and shakes her head. "I'm not angry with you, Vincent. Unfortunately, you're too charming to hate, something I think you're well aware of and use to your advantage. The fact is, I like you...a lot, and I don't know what to do with those feelings. We will get along just fine, don't worry. Just let me get my work done and don't try to get me to do backflips out of a helicopter or whatever."

I laugh and make my way towards the door. "Thank you, Alison. I promise to stay out of your way and let you focus and work without my banal drivel. Now, I'll let you get on with your evening. Thank you for your time, and I hope you sleep well."

I let the door shut behind me and then lean against it...how the hell am I going to ever deserve her? I have to prove to her that I am more than just another rich playboy trying to use her for fun. It was a comment I deserved, and I see why she felt that way. It bothers me that she has mentioned a few times now that she thinks I see her as just another one of my flings. I would do whatever it takes to prove to her that I am worthy of her. Still, the fact that she admitted that she likes me has my stomach doing backflips with excitement.

* * *

TRUE TO MY WORD, I give Alison plenty of space while in Colorado. Like before, she worked around the clock getting the renovations started. As much as I loved watching her work, she needed to have some downtime.

I did manage to persuade her to take me up on an offer to go for a hike. She certainly wasn't used to the altitude and was convinced she would die halfway through, but I made sure to keep the pace slow and controlled for her. The conversation between us was mostly about work; I could tell she was uneasy and not sure where the boundaries were.

By the time the week came to a close, I was ready to get back home. Alison seemed ready as well; she kept mentioning a massage and bottle of wine that were calling her name. She deserved it...she deserved everything.

Now I have to survive the two-and-a-half-hour flight back to Chicago, and then on to Hawaii.

* * *

I CALLED AHEAD to the hotel in Hawaii long before the flight landed on the island. This trip was the first time the two of us traveled together since going to Denver a few weeks ago, and I was taking a chance at putting the two of us in one of the villas on the beachfront in the resort instead of getting Alison her own bungalow separate from mine in the main hotel.

I have no idea about how she was going to react, but if it is anything like the way she reacted back on the roof in Denver, it is going to be an interesting weekend at least. I know she said she wanted space and for things to remain professional between us, and I agreed, but fuck it. I can't keep my word.

I want to do this right. She isn't one of the girls who chases after a man. She deserves to be treated with respect and admiration, and I don't want her to think I am just after one thing. I am after a lot more than just a one-night stand.

I want everything with Alison: the whole package. Everything else in my life besides business has always been about a good time or an adrenaline rush. This is different. There is an adrenaline rush, but it is nothing like what I am used to. I am nervous and excited; my heart races when I think about her, and I ache when she isn't around.

Elise laughed when I called her and told her about what had happened in Denver. I didn't know whether to thank her or blame her for at least some of what happened, even more so when Nate told me that she'd been the one who drove Alison out to the airport right before their Denver trip. There must have been a reason she'd agreed to go out with me so readily. I knew that the two of them had become friends and that they'd been hanging out a lot recently.

I just hope that she isn't going to freak out on me when she finds out the two of us are sharing a villa. We each will have our own room, I wouldn't put that much pressure on her, but the option was there if she decided that was what she wanted. As we check in and the porter shows us to the villa, I see the look on her face, and it causes me to hold my breath.

I don't know her well enough to gauge her expression right now, and I am scared to ask until the porter leaves.

"I hope it's alright that we're sharing the villa. You have a room, and so do I. But if you want me to, I'll go have them put me in another villa on the other side of the island." I am confident about what I am saying, but I am not sure if I am trying to convince her or myself.

Alison turns around and takes a few steps before answering. Her brows are knit together as she looks around the room and notes the bedroom doors on opposite sides of the living area.

"No, it's fine. I wasn't expecting it, but it's perfect. Who wouldn't want to be in a beachfront villa in Hawaii, right?" She sounds a lot less convincing than I had. She is less than thrilled about all of it. The only thing stopping her from walking out is the fact that she could put two doors between us if she decided to.

At least she is going to spend time with me. It is the thing that I have been looking forward to since I started putting the plans for this weekend into place. I don't even recognize myself anymore! Since when do I crave just hanging out with a woman rather than trying to bed her? It is Friday, and I know she has work to do while we are here. But I intend to make sure that she has a good time while we are here, too.

There are a million things I could do that I would enjoy—surfing, mountain climbing, hang gliding across a volcano—but I am pretty sure most of those things aren't Alison's idea of fun. And none of them are conducive to what I have planned.

Thankfully, I had a little help on this front. I won't admit it to Alison, but I might have called her sister Janelle to ask for some advice here. I figured that no one knew her like her little sister, and Elise had been kind enough to make sure I got her number and the two of us were in contact as soon as I'd asked for help. Plans were in motion ever since to make sure that tonight was absolutely on point.

I let Alison go about exploring the hotel and grounds without me, to get a feel for how things worked around here. I want her to get as much of the preliminary work done as possible before dinner tonight, but I make sure to move over to her side as she walks away and whisper in her ear before she goes out the door.

"Dinner is at eight. Don't be late." She shakes her head as she walks out, but her response gives me a glimmer hope.

"Wouldn't miss it for the world." The reply is dripping with sarcasm, but there is something underneath it that she is trying to hide. I also can't help but notice the way her body still reacts to me when my arm lightly brushes against her own. She tenses, the tip of her tongue darting out to nervously lick her lower lip as she tries to mask her reaction.

I almost lose track of time when I notice the sun setting. It is my cue to head back to the villa, take a shower, and get ready for the night.

After the shower, I pull on some casual clothes, grabbing a Hawaiian-print shirt from the top of my suitcase. I smile to myself as I button up the shirt. I know it is completely out of character for me to wear something so outrageous, but I hope it shows my fun, relaxed state.

I move into the kitchen to put the bottle of champagne I've been chilling into a bucket of ice and carry it out to the private patio. Everything has been set up out here for the night. The dinner I had prepared and sent to the villa sits on a table under a warmer with candles under the small cabana that overlooks the beach. The sound of the waves echoing is only interrupted by the sound of the front door of the villa opening and Alison calling out my name.

ALISON

"I'm outside," Vincent calls to me through the open sliding glass door. I make my way towards the lanai, curious as to what's gotten into him.

"Vincent...seriously?" I begin to protest, but he interrupts

"I wanted to. Now take a shower and get comfortable. We're going to spend the evening just the two of us and a private beach, if that's all right with you."

I nod and laugh, brushing my hair back off my forehead.

"I should know better than to argue. Besides, it's been a long day. Just give me a few minutes to grab a shower and change clothes, and then I'm all yours for the rest of the night." I pause for a moment, realizing how that must have sounded.

The last few weeks have been crazy. Right before the trip to Hawaii, I finally got the nerve to clear all of my things out of the apartment Brian and I shared. He had begged and pleaded with me to stop. To stay and reconsider.

He had told me that he never meant to hurt me, that Bridgette had seduced him and had been flirting with him for months. He was scared and didn't know what to do...that was his excuse. Instead of coming to me about what was going on, he gave in to a woman that supposedly meant nothing to him.

I had cried for days, realizing that he threw away years of love and loyalty for nothing. That's how little I meant to him.

It feels nice to be doted on, to be flirted with and desired...even if it is by a playboy billionaire. As much as I don't want to admit it, maybe a good rebound is precisely what I need. To get lost in someone who wants me back.

When I finally re-emerge with hair still wet from the shower in a simple black skirt and tank top, a huge grin spreads across his face.

He stands up, pulling a chair out for me, helping me into my seat and making sure I have a full glass of champagne in front of me before he moves back to his place.

"So, want to play a little game?" He grins across the table at me as I take a bite of the delicious dinner he has prepared.

"A game?" I raise an eyebrow, fully expecting him to suggest strip poker or Twister.

"Yes, a game. You do know Twenty Questions, right? We take turns asking each other questions. Sort of like truth or dare without the dare. So are you up for it?" It looks like he is trying not to sound too eager as he sips his champagne, waiting for my response.

I toy with the top of my glass for a moment as I think about my reply. I reach down, wrapping my fingers around the stem and bringing it up to my lips to drain the glass in one long swig.

"Alright, then. Let's play." I grin, reaching for the bottle from the bucket of ice at the tableside, moving to fill the glass before he begins talking.

"Me first. So, what is your favorite childhood memory?"

I only take a moment to think before I reply, "Building a treehouse with my father when I was nine. He let me use the hammer even though I kept banging him across the thumb every time he held the nails for me." I laugh at the memory and take another drink of champagne.

"What's your favorite color?"

Vincent grins. "That's an easy one. Blue, and I swear it's only a coincidence that your eyes are blue."

I can't help but roll my eyes a little.

Before we hit question ten, Vincent is pouring out his life story to me over our half-forgotten dinner. I am not sure if this is something he shares with many people; some of it is public knowledge, but the details are heartbreaking.

He explains how his grandfather had been the one to push him to go to college. How he'd wanted him to be more than a farmer even though that was what his grandfather had spent all of his adult life doing. He wanted more for his only grandchild. Vincent's mother had come and gone from his life, appearing just long enough to do damage and then disappear again, until they'd gotten word that she'd died in her sleep halfway across the country in a Vegas hotel. It was hard for him to miss someone he'd barely known.

I am captivated by his story; most people in his situation would have given up and become a product of society. He worked damn hard to get where he is. I return the favor by telling him about my own life. My childhood hadn't been nearly as eventful, and my parents had always been a huge part of my life, but I'd been determined not to let them pay a dime to get me through school.

We almost lose track of the number of questions when I realize we are on the last one. By this time, we've completely forgotten about our dinner, and the effects of the champagne are showing on both of us.

He's watching me with a distinct look in his eye. The kind that makes my stomach flip flop.

"Will you kiss me?"

"You mean again?" I drain my glass of champagne.

"Yes, again. Don't tell me you didn't enjoy it before." He keeps his eyes trained on mine; no matter how much I want to try to avoid his gaze and this part of the conversation, I can't.

I let out a frustrated groan, picking up my glass and noticing that it's empty before setting it back on the table. "I was out of my mind, okay? That's the only explanation for it."

"So, someone would have to be out of their mind to kiss me? I'm sure there are going to be a lot of women who are surprised to find that one out."

"Maybe...no. I don't know. I was trying to be spontaneous and 'live in the moment.'" I roll my eyes again as I use overly dramatic air quotes to emphasize my sarcasm.

Vincent stands up, walking around the table to where I sit. He takes my hand to pull me up out of the chair. I'm a little surprised at his sudden movements, but not as surprised as when he pulls me against his hard chest, crashing his lips against mine.

I pull away. "What about the whole giving me space? Keeping a working relationship thing?"

He flashes that cocky grin, knowing he is getting to me with the games he is playing. That had been his goal all along.

I half growl and try to walk away, but he pulls me in again and kisses me once more, hands splayed across my back.

"Why do you keep fighting this, Alison?"

This time he stays put until my body melts into his. He knows what I want, even if I don't. This time when he pulls away, I'm the one to grab his shirt and pull him back in for another kiss.

My brain has completely abandoned me tonight. At least it has completely shut down the second time I kiss him. As much as I want to tell myself that I hate him, there is an equally loud part of my brain that wants him.

I want to get lost in him, let him use my body however he sees fit... this is so unlike me, but I am tired of fighting it.

I don't know what came over me, but I pull him into the bedroom. I want it; there is no doubt. However, I am never impulsive. I am done getting lost in those kisses and stopping there, only having my fantasies to push me over the edge. I need to get lost in every part of him.

I let my lips move against his, my tongue tangling with his own as a soft moan escapes my lips.

My back slams into the wall as Vincent pushes me against it roughly. The cool pressure of it against my back takes my breath away. My fingers fumble with his buttons. I moan again as his lips find my throat. He scrapes his teeth along the gentle curve where it meets my shoulder, biting me firmly for only a second.

I gasp when he tugs my shirt up over my head, dropping it down to the floor before his lips claim mine again. I am not letting him away from me long enough to feel the cool air of the villa hit my skin.

He hooks his fingers in the waistband of my skirt, pulling it down my thighs till it pools at my feet. He steps back and looks me over, licking his lips like he's about to devour me. He places a hand on either side of my face as he leans in and runs his tongue up my neck before whispering in my ear.

"By the time I'm done with you, sweetheart, this whole fucking island will need a cigarette."

18

VINCENT

"You are so fucking beautiful, Alison." I murmur the words against her neck as I nip and lick my way up to her ear. She smells fresh and clean. I flick her earlobe with my tongue before gently sucking it into my mouth, pulling a gasp from her lips.

Her body is still pressed firmly against mine as I pin her to the wall. I reach one hand down her body to feel the soft skin on her thigh. I drag my fingertips slowly upward until they touch the apex. She moans again as I gently brush against her, over her sheer panties. I have to see her, to taste her, to fuck her. I want to consume her in every way possible.

I step back from her; her hand darts out to grab my shirt, but I brush it away. A look of confusion washes over her face.

"I want to see you, baby. All of you," I say as I reach behind her, unclasping her bra. I slide the straps down her slender arms as I watch her full, perky tits spring free. Her nipples are already hard, pert and pink and waiting for me to taste them.

I lean down and flick one with my tongue before popping it into my mouth. Her hands dart up and clutch my hair as her head falls back, and my name tumbles from her lips.

My cock is straining at my shorts, begging to be freed. As if she knows what I'm thinking, one of her hands reaches between us and grabs me firmly through the material. I'm about to explode.

"Vincent...I—I want..."

"Mmmm? What do you want, Alison? Tell me," I tease her as I continue my assault on her delicious breasts. Dragging my lips from one to the other before settling on my knees in front of her.

"I know what I want," I say as I lick my lips and run my nose against her sex. A strangled gasp falls from her mouth as I hook my thumbs in her panties and drag them down her legs. I can smell her; my mouth waters with anticipation as I glance up to meet her eyes.

"Is this what you want?" I say before darting my tongue out to lick her slit. She's sticky with desire already. The taste of her on my tongue sends me into a full frenzy. Before she can respond, I dive face first into her slick mound. Lapping and kissing at her like I'm starving.

Her hands tangle in my hair again as her hips buck forward against my tongue. I reach around behind her and squeeze her ass, pressing her against me even harder.

I can feel her pleasure building as her legs begin to shake, and she pulls at my hair even harder. It stings, but I love it. Knowing that she's about to cum, knowing that I'm the one that's giving her this pleasure.

She pulls one last time before squeezing her thighs against my shoulders, a garbled version of my name shouting from her lips.

Her breathing is labored as she stares down her body, her eyes still full of lust. Before I can register it, she's pulling me up her, crashing her lips against mine as she grabs either side of my shirt and pulls it apart, sending buttons scattering across the tile floor.

We are consumed with one another. I slip my hands into her hair as my tongue massages hers.

"I want you. More," is all she can manage to get out between kissing and pulling my shorts and boxers down my thighs. I move my hands to her waist, lifting as she wraps her legs around me. We stumble our way through the room, crashing into anything in our way as we make our way to the bed.

My brain tells me to stop, to make sure this is what she wants, but

I don't. I can't risk her backing out now. I know she wants me, and I sure as fuck want her. We've been denying ourselves for so long.

I let her body slide down mine as I lower her onto the bed, not keeping us separated for long as I climb over her. I trail kisses up her flat stomach, nipping her breasts before settling myself between her thighs.

Her body feels better than I could have ever imagined. Her breasts feel so soft against my naked chest; the way her hips press against mine causes my dick to twitch and pulse between us. I need relief soon, or I'm going to embarrass myself.

I reach over into the bedside table and pull out a condom, hopeful she won't ask questions about why I put them there. A pretty big assumption on my part but I didn't want to risk any reason why we couldn't be together. She watches as I stretch it over my thick, hard cock. Her eyes are wide, and I can see her swallow hard.

"Don't worry, sweetheart; we'll fit it all in there." I'm not exactly small, and I've seen that look from women in the past. I reach forward and run my finger up her slit again, watching a chill run through her body.

She doesn't take her eyes off mine as I continue to rub my finger back and forth until her wetness is coating it. Her eyelids become heavier as her thighs fall open, exposing her sweet pink pussy to me.

I lean forward, not able to resist, and lick her, stopping to flick her bud with my tongue. I thrust a finger inside her, feeling how tight she is.

"Ohhhh, baby, you're tight. This might be a harder fit than I realized." It doesn't stop me, though. I place the tip of my cock at her entrance and thrust gently. Her mouth pops open as she props herself up on her elbow and watches me.

I grip the base of my length and being to move my hips in small rocking motions, getting her used to the intrusion.

"Am I hurting you?"

She bites her bottom lip and shakes her head, "No...no, it's just been a while." The last word hitches in her throat as I thrust harder. I can feel her start to loosen up as she reaches for me.

I lean my head down so my lips are touching her ear and whisper, "I haven't stopped imagining this since the airport. Wondering how you'd taste, the sounds that would fall from those delicious lips as I pumped into you."

I can see the lust in her eyes as she listens to my words. She pulls me to her mouth and begins to kiss me. Her lips are like pillows: soft and full. The kiss is slow and passionate; it's like a fucking tease as I continue to thrust shallowly into her tight center. Soon, I can't handle it anymore.

My movements become more intentional as I thrust harder and harder until I can feel her pussy gripping me in my entirety. "Oh fuck, Alison…fuck me, you feel so good."

I grunt as I can feel my balls slapping against her with the force of my thrusts. We're both panting as I suck on one of her nipples, biting it until I feel her begin to squeeze me even tighter.

I'm on the edge, and so is she. We're both lost in this moment, lost in each other's bodies. I pull back and grab her hands, pinning them above her head as I thrust again and again until she's screaming my name and arching her back in complete orgasmic bliss.

I shout her name as I pour myself inside her. Gripping her wrists and falling on top of her in a sweaty, satisfied heap.

19

ALISON

Mexico wasn't originally on the itinerary, but Vincent managed to convince me to add it. I still don't see how I can fit it into the design plan and meet the deadlines, but he told me it was more of a preliminary visit. We could get to all of the details and deadlines later.

It has been a week and half since we'd come home from Hawaii. The morning after I woke up in the same bed as him, I panicked. He could see the concern on my face as well as the weird energy that was radiating off of me the rest of the trip.

He told me not to worry about it, that we were just two adults that gave into our desires and he wouldn't read into it. Weirdly, that did little to calm my nerves or make me feel better. The fact that I was falling in love with him was becoming more and more evident to me every day.

The rest of our Hawaii trip was uneventful...well except for the casual sex we had on the veranda the next morning...oh, and in the hammock on the beach. It was like once I had a taste of him, I couldn't walk away. I didn't want to walk away. I just kept telling myself what Janelle had told me: it's just fun, nothing more.

The look on Elise's face when I told her about Hawaii had been priceless. She was clearly guilty of planning half of what had transpired to get the two of us together, and the I-told-you-sos weren't going to stop any time soon. I told her not to read into it; we had simply come to an agreement to enjoy each other's bodies until the hotel renovations were complete. The look she gave me told me she wasn't convinced; it was the same look I gave myself every time I tried saying it meant nothing.

* * *

THE PLANE LANDED at the Cancun International Airport before I realized how long we'd been in the air. I had about a gallon of anticipation and excitement churning in my stomach as the plane touched down. I look over at Vincent to see him smiling wildly at me.

"What's with the face?"

"Nothing, just excited to be here is all. It's one of my favorite locations."

We disembark and make our way toward the waiting car. I can't help but notice the baggage handler taking our luggage in a different direction.

"Vincent, what's going on? Where are our bags going?" I point toward the man who loads them into another car.

That big stupid grin is back on his face.

"Well, I know you've never seen Mexico before, so I arranged a bit of a sightseeing expedition. Let's call it a little adventure. Tell me you brought your bathing suit?"

"I should have known." I shake my head and brush my hair back off my forehead with an exasperated sigh. "So, what is it? You going to make me go skydiving into a pool of molten lava or something?"

He shakes his head and steals a kiss before pulling away and taking my hand to show me to the car.

"Of course not. I know you're not a fan of heights, so I went for something low." The look he shoots me is mischievous, and I can't avoid the playful tone his voice takes on as he asks, "How do you feel about caves?"

"Caves?" Images of bats and stalagmites pop into my head. "I can't say that I've ever even been in a cave."

"Well, I promise you're going to enjoy yourself. Your swimsuit is in the car. I snagged it before we left Chicago."

"Let me guess...Janelle? Elise?" I roll my eyes; as sweet as they are, they are wildly overstepping boundaries.

"So we're going cave swimming. All right. I know zero about caves, so why don't you tell me what you have planned? Then maybe my anxiety-ridden self can enjoy this trip."

He laughs and shakes his head. "Well, we are heading to the cenotes. Normally you have to rappel or base jump into them to get to the bottom, but I may have just found one that has steps carved into the walls so we can get to the bottom without too much fuss. You game?"

"Oh, I'm definitely game." I am actually terrified and full of shit but also not about to let him see that.

The drive out to Ik-Kil takes a couple of hours. Vincent makes the best of the ride by teasing me all the way there, telling me exactly how far down the water is at the bottom. The trees here are ancient, and the entire place has that earthy smell that always comes with somewhere that is home to so many plants.

But it is the giant opening in the ground that is the most astonishing feature of this place. The steps that wind around the inner walls of the sinkhole are a little intimidating since they have no guard rail on the side, but the fall is into a beautiful turquoise pool of water, making it less scary and more of a thrill.

This isn't the kind of thing that I usually would find on my own, but it is breathtaking. For all of his wild ways and crazy stunts, Vincent has completely outdone himself bringing me here. The most exciting 'date' I've been on before was to Six Flags with Brian for my college graduation.

I am awe-struck at the sight of it, even if I am nervous and clinging onto his hand with every step that we take until we reach the diving platform just a few feet above the beautiful clear water.

I don't know what comes over me, but I look over at him and grin.

"Last one in is a rotten egg." It is only a moment before I dive into the water with a gentle squeal, and he follows in soon after. We surface at the same time, and Vincent lunges at me, causing me to laugh and splash him to get away.

"I guess I'm the rotten egg." Vincent finally gets close enough to dive under the water and pull me down with him. Surfacing before me, he watches me bob up, sputtering for air. It takes me a moment to cough all of the sea water out of my nose before I glare over at him.

"I don't know about rotten eggs, but you're an asshole, Vincent."

He grasps his chest dramatically, pretending to be hurt.

"You wound me, Alison. Here I am just trying to be friendly and show you the sights around Mexico, and you call me an asshole. I'm hurt. Really..." He flashes me that colossal grin, wagging his eyebrows at me until I splash him again.

The two of us spend the afternoon swimming until we are both exhausted and wind up laying face-up on the diving platform, staring at the sky and cave ceiling above. Vines hang down into the opening with leaves, holding birds that come and go in flocks as the sun moves above us.

I lay there with my head on the rock ledge, looking up at the sky as the light filters in through layers of green and blue that reflect around us. Vincent reaches over and pulls me to rest against his shoulder instead of the hard surface of the rock.

"So, I bet you bring all the girls here."

"Actually, you'd be the first." I sit up surprised.

"Seriously?"

"Yeah, seriously. I never took anyone else out here. I don't think I've taken anyone out here but Nate, and as much fun as the two of us have together, Nate's just not as pretty as you are, and he certainly doesn't fill out a bikini like you do."

"So you're telling me you haven't come out here with any of those actresses or supermodels you like to hang out with?" I narrow my eyes intently, studying his face as if trying to catch him in a lie, not sure why I care.

"Never. They're way more interested in the boutique hotel I

opened up just off Rodeo Drive or the one in Manhattan than they are about exploring Mexico and swimming in water that hasn't been through about a million pool filters. Besides, swimsuits that cost more than a semester of college tuition aren't meant to get wet."

I raise my eyebrows in surprise. "I guess I should be flattered then."

"Trust me, Alison. I'm the one that's flattered. Besides, I get to see you in that swimsuit. It was well worth the drive."

I move to hit his arm, but he uses the opportunity to lean in and steal another kiss from my lips. I stand up almost immediately, and Vincent moves to join me.

"Listen, Alison I..." I don't know where this conversation is going but am not ready to spoil this moment. I lean forward and push against his chest, sending him backward. I double over in laughter at the look of pure shock that registers on his face right before he hits the water.

20

VINCENT

Alison is waiting on me when I walk into the bedroom we are sharing back at the hotel. Today has been both amazing and frustrating. The memory of sharing something so beautiful with Alison will stick with me forever.

It is a little surreal that she's been spending so much time with me, even though it seems like I get on her nerves ninety percent of the time. I was hopeful that I could talk to her today about what is going on between us, but she clearly wasn't in the mood since she pushed me into the water.

I didn't want to ruin things, so I took the hint. A big reason I added Mexico to the trip list was because I couldn't handle the thought of our relationship ending after Iceland. I wasn't ready to let her go.

I can't read her yet. I don't know if this all means nothing to her. Me? I am falling...fast and hard.

I step out of the shower, wrapping a towel around my waist as I move into the bedroom.

"Holy shit!" I stop dead in my tracks at the sight of Alison spread out across the bed, dressed in nothing but barely there lingerie

"Well...I wasn't expecting that. You look amazing!" I let my eyes trail down her body, taking in every little detail. I can see her pink nipples through the white lace and the small, dark thatch of curls behind the matching panties.

"I hope so. All of this was pretty expensive."

I let out a small laugh as I walk around the bed to admire her. She rolls from her side to her stomach, exposing the G-string that runs up her delicious ass. I run my hand over my stubble-lined jaw, clenching my teeth in anticipation.

"You did a good job. It's a shame that I'm not going to let it stay on that long, but I'm sure it'll look almost as good on the floor."

Alison curls a finger and pushes herself back further on the bed to summon me over to her, but as I began to move over her, she leans up and pushes me onto my back. Something about the outfit she is wearing has gone to her head, and she is feeling like taking things over for herself this time.

"Nuh uh…" Alison moves to grab the towel from around my waist, pulling it off, tossing it to the floor. "It's my turn, Mr. Crawford."

Fuck! Hearing her call me that has me rock hard and ready to beg for her to take me in her mouth.

I lay back, placing my hands under my head to glance at her with a sly grin.

"Fair enough, Alison. I promise to be patient."

She moves over to stand next to the bed, dragging the nail of her index finger along my upper thigh and over my hip with a wink.

"I promise that you're going to be far from patient by the time I get done with you." Her nails stop their path as she leans in to steal a kiss and move to position herself straddling my thighs, arms draping over my shoulders as she settles her weight onto my body.

She is taking her time, moving slowly against me as the two of us kiss with her fingers tangled in my hair. She tugs at it, nipping at my lower lip, drawing a groan from my mouth. My hands move to her hips to guide her motions until I stop her with a low growl.

"Fuck patience. I want you. Now."

My voice is gravelly with desire, almost unrecognizable. It is a quick motion to move her body and position herself astride me; she leans over to the bedside table and grabs a condom, stretching it over my pulsing manhood. The full length of my cock is waiting at the opening of her pussy as she sinks onto it with a low moan.

She presses her hands against my chest as she begins to piston herself up and down my length. This is going to be quick. I'm grunting, thrusting my hips up every time she comes down on me. She changes the motion, grinding down hard on me as she swivels her hips and throws her head back. Her tits bounce with every move, and we're both on the edge.

I grasp her a little more roughly, moaning with her as we both come together. My hands never leave her body, even when she begins moving against me, nails digging lightly into the plane of my chest as she uses her arms for leverage. My hand guides her every motion, and my eyes lock with hers.

"God, you're beautiful, Alison." I stare at her, my eyes taking in every inch. It is absolutely intoxicating to see watch her movements, seeing her confidence as she just lets her body control it all.

She continues to move as my cock hardens inside her. I need more. I wrap her in my arms, moving beneath her to keep the high from her orgasm going as I hold her still and use my hips to bring her to the brink of orgasm once again. My name is just a gentle whisper on her lips, but I want to hear it louder.

"Say it again, Alison. Say my name. Fuck, I love the way it sounds."

This time she moans it loudly, thrusting her hips into mine in the same moment that she finds her release. Her nails dig more roughly into the skin of my shoulder blades. Her body shaking gently as a climax grasps ahold of her and rocks her until she goes limp against my chest.

"That's my girl," I growl as I begin to thrust harder, taking what I want. What I need.

"Please, Vincent…" Her voice is breathless.

"Please what?"

"God…" Her breath comes in a gasp as her head falls back onto the bed. "I want to feel you cum."

I moan as my length twitches inside her, my hands pinning her hips to the bed, slamming deep into her one last time as she cries out along with me.

21

ALISON

The plane is just about to touchdown back at O'Hare as I stir in my seat. I am exhausted from another whirlwind week of work on top of passionate, hot sex. I never realized the limits that my body could handle...Vincent pushed me emotionally and physically past anything I had ever experienced. It was exhilarating and invigorating; my body craved his touch even when I knew I was completely depleted. He had explored every single inch of my body with his hands and mouth—kissing, licking, and biting his way across my flesh.

I have no idea what's happening. We both agreed it would be casual, with no intentions, but it's hard to believe that with the way he looks at me. I almost kick myself for getting involved with him.

I'm trying to be optimistic and open-minded, but I also know with Vincent's past, there is a high probability this is nothing more than a long fling. I am also trying to convince myself that this is what I want; I am young and on the rebound.

An image of Brian flashes across my mind. I still feel guilty about how I ended things with him. We both said some hurtful things, but it was like he still had a small hold on me. I didn't love him anymore, but I missed what we had. I was still hurt and angry that he ruined something I'd poured my heart into and threw away like it was garbage.

"Alison, sweetheart?" Vincent gently runs his hand over my arm, waking me out of my daze.

I stir in my seat to see Vincent leaning over me. "We're about to land." He leans down and gently presses a soft kiss to my lips.

How could a moment like this be fake? The tender way he brushed the hair off my forehead and planted a kiss on my lips couldn't just be for sex, could it? I shake my head clear of the thoughts and remind myself that Brian too made me feel loved and safe and look how that turned out.

* * *

I am glad to be home. I need some time and space to clear my head from Vincent. Put things into perspective and prepare for this last trip to Iceland. I have some final decisions that still have to be made for each location; thankfully, I can manage it all from my office here. I want to touch base with Madeline and give her a progress update on everything so far.

I feel exhausted but also…invigorated. I flop back dramatically on my bed, staring up at the ceiling. I let my mind wander to Vincent. I know I'm falling for him.

Once I removed the judgments I had about him, I was free to see the real Vincent, not the façade he put on for others. There was no condescension in his words; he praised me continuously and built me up. This is the kind of man I want and need. He encourages me to be bold and try new things, to embrace life as Janelle does so freely.

There is only one reason I am fighting my feelings for him…well, two. I can't help but think of his past…first, would I just be another woman that he would tire of eventually? And second, would he even want an actual relationship? Maybe this is all Vincent Crawford can offer.

"Ugh, I need wine." I pour myself a glass and pick up the phone to call Janelle.

Janelle listens intently as I pour out my heart to her. "The funny thing is I didn't see this coming, Elle! I swear! I know I can be overly type-A and regimented, but I did take your advice and told myself I would live in the moment and enjoy this for what it is...I never expected anything to come of it."

Janelle can't help but laugh on the other end of the phone. "Ali, sometimes living in the moment and enjoying what comes your way is exactly how you change your life and fall in love. That's the best kind of love there is: purely organic!"

"I didn't say *love*, Janelle; it's just...puppy love at the moment. Maybe it's just me feeling better about myself since getting cheated on by Brian."

"No! Do not self-sabotage and do not allow that infected asshole to ruin this for you! Ali, I love you, but you could easily sabotage your entire existence with 'what ifs.' When I said live in the moment and embrace what the universe has sent your way, I didn't mean embrace it until it becomes uncomfortable or uncertain and then bail. Life doesn't work like that. Look, you're insanely smart and gifted, but if all you ever do is think about the negative 'what ifs,' you could miss out on the greatest happiness in life...the next time you think about what if this could fail, think about what if this turns out to be everything you've ever wanted in life."

I sit in silence. "Seriously, Elle, how are you so wise? I'm astounded at the truth and insight that comes out of your mouth sometimes. You're so right. I need to do what's right for me and not hold back because of the unknown. That's not fair to me. God, I love you so much. I don't know where I'd be without you."

I hang up the phone and make the decision that hiding away from Vincent and my feelings isn't worth the regret that could come with it. Nope, starting tomorrow, I am going to be open to what the universe has for me and embrace it.

22

VINCENT

Iceland had always been one of the places where I wanted to own a hotel. I'd read about it in one of the books I lugged home from the library as a little boy. The volcanoes and hot springs were fascinating. As an adult, more than that had drawn me to the area. So when the opportunity to acquire property there presented itself, I jumped at the chance. The fact that it was one of the resorts adjacent to some of the most famous hot springs in the world just sweetened the deal.

Bringing Alison with me to look over the resort for the first time was the icing on the cake. The thought that the woman I loved would leave her artistic fingerprints all over my hotels was exciting. I'd never met someone who not only made me completely reinvigorated for life but also made me want to be a better man.

This place was going to be one of her favorites. I just knew that the surroundings were going to be a world of inspiration for her, and I was going to get a chance to do something I'd always wanted to do. Surfing in the icy waters there, surrounded by snow and chunks of icebergs, was going to be a first for me. Alison wasn't a surfer, but she'd agreed to come along and watch, getting some pictures and recording me in action.

The entire island was fairly small, and the drive from the airport to the hotel was blissfully short. We had plenty of time to settle in before we headed out to see the rest of the resort.

I had some work to get done, and she needed to get some photos of the resort, as well as measurements. We both agreed to meet back at the room in a few hours to enjoy the hot springs before dinner.

The hot springs are only a quick walk from the resort. There is a section reserved only for the hotel guests apart from the public springs that were always packed with people. Since the introduction of social media, this place has become a bit of a tourist trap. The private springs are a little more secluded, and as we arrive, we are the only two guests there.

She's wearing the same swimsuit she wore in Mexico, only this time she is wrapped under a bathrobe to ward off the chill in the air. The water is amazingly blue, so much so that it almost looks artificial beneath the low cloud of steam that sits over the water. It is the only indication of how warm it is inside.

Alison scrambles into the water to avoid the cold air and sighs in relief when she is mostly submerged. I laugh as I watch how adorable she is, removing my robe before slipping in to join her.

"So, what do you think of the place?" I ask.

"Honestly, Vincent, this place needs barely, if any, changes. The Scandinavian design here is perfect for the location, and the clean lines highlight the architecture of the place."

I knew she'd love it. The truth is I knew it really didn't need any changes. I just wanted to bring her here to experience it, to share it with me.

I don't have it all planned out yet, but I am going to tell Alison exactly how I feel tonight. I don't want to scare her away; we both agreed this is all just a good time. She's also just gotten out of a serious relationship, and she's considerably younger than me. Maybe she isn't even looking for something, but I'll never forgive myself if I let her slip away without telling her how I feel.

After dinner, we retire back to our room, relaxing before we make our way out to the beach for my first attempt at surfing the icy waters. One of the only rules when surfing in Iceland is don't surf alone. With the powerful waves and icy conditions, it can be incredibly dangerous.

Alison excuses herself to the use bathroom just as her phone buzzes on the nightstand next to me. I don't know why I pick it up, but I see Brian's name on the screen with the preview of a text message that reads,

I miss you baby...can't stop thinking about you.

My stomach drops. I feel like I just got kicked in the balls. Like a glutton for punishment, I swipe my finger across the screen to unlock it as she emerges from the bathroom.

She's smiling, but it fades as soon as she sees the look on my face. "What's wrong?" Then she glances at my hand where I'm holding her phone.

"What are you doing? Are you going through my phone?"

I toss it on the bed and stand up. "No, obviously not, since you have a passcode." I don't know why I say it like that; everybody has a passcode on their phone.

"Why did you have it in your hand, Vincent?" Anger flashes in her eyes.

"Because it buzzed on the nightstand when you got up to use the bathroom. I don't know; I thought it was mine or something. I just grabbed it."

She says nothing, just stares silently at me. "You've got a text from your fiancé," I say passive aggressively as I hand it back to her. I hate who I am at this moment. She doesn't deserve this.

"My ex-fiancé," she shouts back at me, emphasizing the ex. "Why is he my fiancé again all the sudden?"

"Well, clearly there's unfinished business there, Alison. You're leading one or both of us on." I'm making ridiculous accusations now because I'm hurt. Why can't I give her the benefit of the doubt and let her explain it?

"Leading you on? How? You are the one who said this was all just for fun and to let loose. We both agreed to those conditions, so how is that leading you on? You have prided yourself on being this playboy who fucks anyone and everyone!" Her words cut like a knife, mostly because she's right but also because I realize I'm nothing more to her than a good-time fuck, just like I told I should be.

"Don't throw that at me now Alison, we both know that's not what this is anymore." I spit out the words as I gesture between us.

"Seriously? So now I'm just supposed to know what you're feeling and that things have changed like I'm some kind of god damn mind reader?"

"Is he what you want? Is this it?" I gesture toward the phone that is now in her hands.

She looks down at it. "No. And it's not what you think at all." She is still angry and has every right to be. She just told me exactly what I want to hear, but instead of going to her and confessing my love for her, I storm out of the room, grabbing my surf bag, and make my way to the beach.

Compared to the warmth of the hot springs where we had just spent the better part of the afternoon, the waters at the shore are bracing and icy. There are chunks of ice floating in the water and sitting on the beach that are bigger than a Buick. The sun is low in the sky, hanging just behind one of the mountains in the distance, and the blue and green colors of the Northern Lights are dancing above me. The sun looks as if it is setting, but this time of year, it is only just going to dip below the horizon and then come back up slowly. The light will never go away completely.

This is the perfect time of year to come out and experience this, and now the memory is tainted. No one else is out on the beach except one or two other daredevils hoping to catch a swell. Rules be dammed, I'm doing this anyway. I need to clear my head.

The waves are huge, pounding into the rocky beach in a rhythmic pattern that has a hypnotic effect on anybody watching. I spend a few minutes studying the pattern of the waves while I wait for the perfect one. They are huge and powerful. I am going to have to catch one just right to avoid being thrown off my board in the attempt, and I want to get this perfect on the first try.

I count the seconds between swells, noting that the third wave of each set is always the largest one, and time my attempt with the way the largest one yet curls over and begins to crash against the icy water below.

I know something is wrong as soon as the current catches my board and pulls me into the curl, but I don't realize quite how out of control I am until I am caught in the tube of the wave, but by then, it is too late, and the next thing I register is the crack of my head against one of the gigantic pieces of rock in the water as the wave drags me under.

23

ALISON

Since coming back from Mexico, it was like my mental clarity about what I wanted was becoming more and more lucid. I knew I was in love with Vincent; I just had to grow enough courage to tell him.

Even after I moved everything out of the apartment I once shared with Brian and told him to fuck off, he still wouldn't accept the fact that we were done. My phone buzzed, and I pulled it out of my pocket to see the message he sent days after I'd moved my stuff out.

Hey, Babe, I know you need space and time, and I'm trying, but I miss you like crazy. I can't stop thinking about you. I hope you're missing me too. I love you so much.

I rolled my eyes and ignored the message, tossing my phone on my bed as I packed for Iceland.

I replayed the last exchange we had, when I moved my stuff out of our old apartment.

"Alison, please! Stop! Stop! I'm begging you!" Brian grabbed at my hands as I pulled my clothes from our dresser and shoved them haphazardly into a suitcase. I wasn't expecting him to be home this soon; he must have dipped out of work early. I, on the other hand, was giving him the silent treatment... immature, but I didn't know how to communicate my feelings at the moment.

I continued packing my things as Brian tore them back out of my suitcase like it was a cartoon. I was beyond frustrated; none of this was going according to plan. He had come home about an hour after I arrived and immediately began to beg and plead with me to stay and hear him out. I could see this was going nowhere, so I finally relented. "Fine, let's hear it."

"What?" He stood speechless for a moment with his fists full of my clothes.

"I'll listen to whatever excuse or story it is that you think will explain why I found you with your dick in Bridgette Trent." I could see him shift nervously from one foot to the other at the mention of her name. "Let's go into the living room." I led the way, stopping to grab a bottle of water from the fridge.

We sat in silence for another few moments once we reached the living room. I could see he was gathering his thoughts as he sat tensely on the edge of the couch. "Look, I know there's no excuse for my behavior. It was a moment born purely out of lust and loneliness and alcohol. I...honestly, she came on to me first."

I rolled my eyes as he tried to excuse his behavior...right after saying there was no excuse for it.

"I swear, Alison; she had been flirting with for months, sending me inappropriate emails and texts!"

"Hold up: this had been going on for months, and you didn't think to share it with me? The woman you loved and were engaged to? Or your boss? If she was sending you emails, you should have gone to your immediate supervisor or HR if you didn't want it, but you didn't! You encouraged it, Brian!" I could feel my pulse rising as I pointed a finger at him.

"I know, I know! I know, Alison! I fucked up, okay!"

"No, you didn't fuck up, Brian; you made a deliberate choice. You chose her over me. Her over us. Over our love and what we built together. The trust, honesty...all gone!" I couldn't hold back any longer, and I burst into tears. I felt like my stomach was going to expel its contents onto the floor, so I made a mad dash to the bathroom.

A few moments later, I could hear what sounded like arguing coming from the other room. I splashed cold water on my face and took a few deep breaths before returning to the living room. "Brian?"

"Alison, come on; we can deal with this later. Did you get anything

packed?" Janelle was making a beeline for me across the floor; I could see her face was red, and Brian stood silently in the background.

"Not really."

She glared at Brian and pointed right in his face. "You stay here and don't move; understand? Your behavior is sickening, and you need to let her get some things and figure shit out, okay?" Brian nodded his head and put his hands in the air as if to surrender.

I made my way to our old bedroom and packed a quick bag of my things before heading back out into the living room where Janelle had Brian cornered. Without a word or even a glance at Brian, I made my way out of the apartment into Janelle's car.

This was exactly the closure I needed. If I thought for one brief second I wanted him back, I wasn't confused any longer. I had avoided picking my things up from Brian's for months. I wasn't sure if I was still secretly holding out hope or if it was just the fact I didn't want to face him. Either way, it was done.

And now here I am, about to lose the main I love over something so stupid. What have I done in all this to make him not trust me?

I'm not angry at Vincent for holding my phone or even going through it if he could have. I am angry that he threw the friends with benefits shit in my face and acted like I betrayed him because my dumbass ex text me. How is this my fault?

I wanted to stop him, but I knew his mind was made up, so I let him storm out. I pick up my phone again, not knowing what time it is back in Chicago but call Janelle anyway.

"Hey, what's up?" Her breathing sounds heavy on the other end of the phone.

"Uh, did I interrupt something? What time is it there?"

"I'm just out running; it's the afternoon here."

I explain the situation to Elle, hoping she can give me a magic answer to fix everything.

"Well, I mean…he doesn't have a right to be pissed at you for that. Even if you were sleeping with someone else, he shouldn't be upset if you guys didn't say you were exclusive. I would tell Brian to go jump up his own ass and die so he gets the message loud and clear, but I'd also be very transparent about it all with Vincent. He clearly has feelings for you, sis. Guys don't get that butthurt if it's just a casual hookup."

I laugh and lean back on the bed; she always knows what I need to hear. "Thanks as always, sis. I'm going to set things straight with Vincent before he does something stupid on the water and hurts himself. I love you; I'll see you when I'm back home."

I toss the phone on the bed with a huge grin on my face and grab my boots and coat and run out the door. I can picture Vincent's face when I shout to him that I love him and demand he make love to me before he hurts himself on the waves.

But I'm too late. Just as I approach the beach, I see him run out into the water and catch a massive wave. His balance is off, and I see him fall, the water catapulting him directly into a giant chunk of ice. I scream his name and run as fast as I can to the water, but he can't hear me. It's freezing, but I don't care. I kick off my boots, throw off my coat, and run into the icy waters, but I can't find him.

ALISON

I was growing used to the sounds of the machines that surrounded Vincent in the hospital room he'd been set up in for the better part of a week. It had gotten to the point that the rhythmic beeping and whirring was enough to lull me off to sleep. It didn't help that I'd barely slept since two fellow surfers helped me pull Vincent from that freezing water back in Iceland.

The water was insanely cold, but I'd barely noticed it in my rush to get him out of the waves. When I watched Vincent go down, my heart had leaped into my throat. I wasn't even sure I remembered how to breathe until I started screaming for help as I struggled to find him.

Everything had been a blur after that. Two fellow surfers appeared out of nowhere and pulled his body from the water. An ambulance had arrived, and the paramedics had seen to the bleeding gash on his forehead while I watched helplessly. I'd gone with him to the hospital, silently praying he would wake up and that everything would be ok while the paramedics also tried to make sure I was all right and not suffering from hypothermia after my dip in the frigid water without a wet suit on. My clothes were still wet when we reached the hospital, but I would only leave his side long enough to change into the scrubs they'd given me when they forced me to leave the room.

The next day, when he'd been airlifted from the hospital to the airport and loaded onto a jet filled with medical staff to be flown back to Chicago, I was expecting him to wake up at any moment. But there wasn't any sign of him even fluttering an eyelid in spite of all the movement.

The doctors cleared him for travel. Since Nate had his power of attorney and a bunch of legal paperwork stating Vincent's wishes to be brought back to Northwestern Memorial in Chicago if anything should happen to him, the doctors released him to his care. They put him a medically induced coma for the trip and to allow the swelling in his brain to decrease.

After arriving back in Chicago, there were scans and tests and monitors and just about every imaginable piece of equipment hooked up to him soon after we arrived. He was breathing on his own. The doctors all said that was a good sign, that there seemed to be no sign of permanent brain damage, but they still hadn't brought him out of the medically induced coma. It was disheartening, but I refused to leave the hospital.

It took a lot of convincing from Janelle and Elise to even talk me into going for food from time to time. The only time I would leave him was when the doctors or Nate were there to take my place. If he was going to be alone, I refused to go. When he woke up, I didn't want him to be confused or afraid. Every night I slept with my head resting on the hospital bed near his hand, so I'd wake up if he did.

It's Friday morning, almost a week since he fell into the water and hit his head on the rocks. I wake as the sunlight streams through the blinds. It won't be long before the room will be flooded with light.

I was up late last night, just talking to Vincent while we were alone. I missed him being able to answer me, but the doctors said he could still hear me. I'd passed out in the middle of mumbling a story about the most embarrassing thing that had happened to me in middle school.

I am still stuck between waking up from the sun and trying to stay asleep a little longer when I feel movement in the bed. I ignore it at first, but when he runs his fingers through the hair that lay haphazardly across my cheek, tucking it behind my ear, my eyes flutter open quickly.

It takes me a moment to remember where I am or that I am here with an injured Vincent. Everything registers all of a sudden, and when I look up to find him awake and grinning down at me in spite of the row of stitches on his temple, I nearly jump straight up and onto the bed beside him.

"Vincent! You're awake!" As soon as the words leave my mouth, I burst into tears. I shout for a nurse as Vincent covers my mouth with his hand.

"I am, but how long have I been out? And where am I?" He looks around for a moment but doesn't hesitate to wrap an arm around me and pull me in closer. "Don't cry, sweetheart; I'm still alive, aren't I?" He winces a little as he reaches up to touch the stitches.

"Five days." I wipe away tears that stream uncontrollably down my cheeks. He knits his brows together, looking concerned.

"And you're back in Chicago at Northwestern Memorial. Nate took care of it all."

He nods, leaning in to press a kiss to my forehead as I carefully move in to be closer to him.

"Then he did exactly what I would have wanted him to do. I didn't break anything, right? My brains aren't scrambled?" He grins a little. It is like him to be trying to joke around at a moment like this.

"Not any more than normal. They had to put you in a medically induced coma until the brain swelling decreased, but I didn't know when you'd be waking up. They must have reduced your medication last night when I was asleep."

"Tell me you haven't been here all five days."

I glance up at him. "Of course. I couldn't leave you alone."

"Tell me you went home and at least grabbed a shower." He groans when I just shake my head.

"It's a good thing I'm in this hospital bed, or I'd do something unspeakable to punish you for that one."

"I wasn't going to go anywhere until I knew you were going to be all right, Vincent. I wasn't going to leave the man I love to wake up alone while I went off to have some luxury shower," I gesture wildly, completely unaware of the words that just tumbled out of my mouth.

"Whoa, whoa...the man you love?"

My heart feels like it stops beating. The words just fell out without me even realizing it.

He grins and steals a kiss. "And who's that lucky son of a bitch?"

"You. For some crazy, insane, self-destructive reason...I love you." I hadn't said it out loud before now, but it feels good to say.

I knew the moment I thought I'd lost him that this wasn't just a no-strings-attached fling. This is it. True, all-encompassing love. I ramble on trying to express myself and explain the text from Brian when he cuts me off, pulling me in for another kiss. This one is long and lingering, his fingers curling around behind my neck to keep me there until he pulls away and takes a soft breath.

"I love you too, Alison. In fact, I had planned to tell you on the beach in Iceland, but it seems my hurt feelings and petulant behavior got better of me first. Can you ever forgive me for behaving that way?"

I catch his eyes, carefully stroking a finger through his hair as I avoid the line of stitches there. I don't want to start crying again so instead of replying, I lean in, planting a kiss on his forehead and letting myself linger there for a moment.

"Well, I've got you speechless, I think. That's got to be a first. I don't know if I should ask you the next thing on my mind or not since I don't know if you'll be able to answer me."

"If you ask me to go on another one of your death-defying acts, I swear to God, Vincent." He laughs, but I am completely serious. I am not certain what is coming next, but the words that come out of his lips are the last thing I ever expected to hear.

"Marry me?" He threads his fingers between mine, holding my hand until he brings it to his lips for a kiss. "And before you protest, I'm not brain damaged or addled. I know what I want. I knew it before I ever got on that surfboard. What I want is you. So just tell me you'll marry me."

I am shocked silent for a moment. It takes me a second to find the words.

I never expected life would take this turn...that when I rattled my way through my first airport meeting with Vincent Crawford, it would end up with both of us falling madly in love. I can't help but remember Janelle's comments from a few weeks ago: 'What if you let go and find out that the what-ifs are everything you've always wanted?' All of this feels right, and there is only one answer I can give.

"Yes, yes, of course, I'll marry you!" Tears begin streaming down my face as I lean in to press my forehead to his. "Just one small thing though...make sure you ask me again after they release you from the hospital, so I know you haven't completely lost your mind."

He laughs and pulls me in for another kiss. "Oh, trust me; I'm going to ask you as often as I can until you finally say 'I do,' and maybe even after. Just to make sure you haven't lost your mind too."

I can't stop smiling. "Just shut up and love me, Vincent Crawford."

He grins against my lips, muttering, "Only for the rest of my life, Alison Ryder."

EPILOGUE

SEVERAL MONTHS LATER...

"See something you like?" Alison can see my reflection in the window in front of her. I don't even know how long I've been standing here staring at her. The golden hue of the sky has created a magical backdrop to her silhouette as she looks at my penthouse window.

"Only the best view in the entire city." I walk up behind her, letting my hand rest on her hip as I use the other to move aside the tumble of curls exposing her neck to my lips.

"Mmmm" a soft moan escapes her mouth as I run my tongue up her silky skin followed by a nip of my teeth. She reaches behind her and grabs my suit coat.

"I have watched you all day flitter about the hotel. Taking notes and pictures, giving instructions to the furniture delivery team. All eyes were on you sweetheart and I just kept thinking to myself, she's all mine. I'm the one who gets to kiss those full lips at the end of the day." I move both of my hands to her hips and let them slide up her body until I cup her firm breasts. "I'm the one who gets to touch these delicious tits, to suck on these little pink nipples." I slip my hand inside her blouse and pull her bra cup down as I pinch her nipple. Her moan turns into a gasp as her head lulls back against my shoulder.

"I'm all yours baby." She says, pushing her ass against my rigid cock. I reach down the front of her and unbutton her blouse as I continue to nip at her neck. I remove the shirt and toss it on the floor followed by her bra.

"Put your hands against the glass." I say, waiting for her to comply. She looks confused for a moment before I lift her hands and press them against the floor to ceiling window.

"Don't move. Understand?" She gives me a subtle nod as her eyeline meets mine in the reflection. I reach between us and unzip her skirt, letting it fall to the floor leaving her in only her panties and heels.

"Fuck me baby, you look like a fantasy." I step back to admire her ass on prominent display as she's bent a little at the waist, her top half still braced against the window by her outstretched arms.

"Vincent please…"

"Please what?" I know it's fucked up but I like it when she begs.

"Please to—touch me." Her voice hitches in her throat as I grab the g-string going up between her firm cheeks and snap it, tossing it to the floor.

"Bend over more." She looks back at me, again with a questioning look on her face.

"Alison, sweetheart, do what I say. I promise I'm going to make it worth your while."

She turns back around and bends over, completely exposing her wet slit to me. I grit my teeth together, I can feel the saliva pooling in my mouth.

I grab a chair and sit it behind her, taking a moment to lean forward and inhale her sweet aroma. I can't take much more, I reach up and slap her ass, watching it bounce and redden a little.

"Agh!" She looks back at me, shocked.

"Did you like it baby?" She bites her bottom lip and nods slowly.

That's all the encouragement I need, I slap her again watching her body lurch forward. This time I follow it up by running my finger up her center. Her knees buckle a little but she catches herself.

I continue this little game a few more times before plunging two fingers deep inside her warm core. She's panting, her arms are no longer straight but her elbows are against the glass as well as one side of her face as she rocks her body back against my fingers. I can feel her begin to tighten around them, I want her to cum in my mouth.

I pull my fingers out only to replace them with my tongue. I grab her ass, spreading her so I can dive in and lap at her with ferocity. She's moaning, trembling, begging for release, finally calling out my name in orgasmic bliss.

"I'm not done with you Alison. Back up and sit on my cock baby." I watch as she pulls herself up from the window, looking back to see me still sitting in the chair stroking myself. It took me about point five seconds to get myself free once I tasted her.

"Trust me this is going to be quick, you get me so turned on. Face the window." I scoot forward in the chair as she places a hand on each armrest before slowly starting to lower herself down.

"Like this?" She teases, letting just the tip inside her entrance before rising back up. "Is this what you want?" I can't even form a thought as I watch her perky little ass start to bounce up and down on me. I let her have her moment of fun, teasing me, before grabbing her hips and forcing her all the way down.

"Oh shit!" She shouts as she grips the arm rest even tighter.

"Unless you're ready to get fucked hard and deep, don't tease me like the Alison." I snake my hand around her chest until it's at the base of her neck. "Now sweetheart, ride me. I want to see you fuck yourself on me."

She doesn't hesitate, she moves up and down my shaft stopping only at the base to grind against me a little deeper. I'm done for. I grip her hips helping her up and down as we both start to tremble. I can feel every muscle in my body tense as I release my load inside her.

"Come on baby, let me take care of you." I mumble in her ear as our breathing subsides. I finish stripping out of the rest of my clothes before picking her up and taking her to the bathroom.

I draw up a bath and we both lower ourselves down into the water. "How was your day? Besides stalking me?" She leans back against my chest as I rub the soapy loofah gently over her body.

"It was busy but I was wildly distracted by you. Watching you is my new favorite hobby. You're like a beautiful, graceful beam of light."

"Well, that goes both ways you know. I can always sense when you're around and it still makes me kind of—nervous? Excited? I still get that symphony of butterflies in my stomach."

I can't help the huge grin that spreads across my face as I lean in to kiss her ear. "I hope that never goes away."

"There is one thing that kept popping in my head today."

"Hmmm? And what was that?" She asks.

"Well, I like knowing you're mine and I'd like everyone else to know it too."

"Vince, I'm pretty sure this insane rock on my hand tells them I'm with someone." She says turning around to flash the five-carat diamond I picked out for her a few months ago.

"I'd love it even more if there was a more obvious tell." I reach down and rub her belly.

"A baby?" She practically shouts, turning around and sending water sloshing over the edge.

"You want to knock me up so people won't what? Hit on me? Take me from you?" I can see this is not going how I had hoped and it's certainly not the reason why.

"No, no Alison honestly, I've just been thinking a lot about us and our life and I want a family with you. I—" I don't want to scare her but the truth is I keep having dreams about it.

"What?"

"I keep having dreams about you as a mom. I just want to give that to you. I want to have a family with you." She looks at me without blinking and then lunges at me, wrapping her arms around my neck.

"I would love to have a family with you too Vincent. I think we're going to be amazing parents, but I also don't want to rush it. I want to enjoy what you and I have right now and focus on the wedding."

"That's perfectly okay with me sweetheart. I just want you to know that should it happen, I am already excited and looking forward to that day. You are the love of my life Alison Ryder."

She leans forward and softly presses her lips against mine. It doesn't take more than thirty seconds for the kiss to deepen. Soon our tongues are exploring each other as our bodies intertwine and she grins herself against me.

"That being said Mr. Crawford, we can certainly practice trying over and over and over again." She whispers in my ear as I stand up with her around my waist, walking us to the bed before tossing her on her back with a squeal.

"In that case Miss Ryder, you better start calling me daddy."

READ THE REST OF THE SERIES HERE

Hate That I Love You: Castille Hotel Series Prequel

Want this prequel for FREE? Sign up here to get it along with a second free novel delivered right to your inbox!

READ THE REST OF THE CASTILLE HOTEL SERIES HERE!

Baby Mistake: Castille Hotel Series Book 2
Fake It: Castille Hotel Series Book 3

ALSO BY ALEXIS WINTER

South Side Boys Series

Damaged-Book 1

Broken-Book 2

Wrecked-Book 3

Redemption-Book 4 (Coming February)

Make Her Mine Series

My Best Friend's Brother

Billionaire With Benefits

My Boss's Sister

My Best Friend's Ex

The Friend Agreement (Coming this March)

Mountain Ridge Series

Just Friends: Mountain Ridge Book 1

Protect Me: Mountain Ridge Book 2

Baby Shock: Mountain Ridge Book 3

Claimed by Him: A Contemporary Romance 6 Book Collection

ALL BOOKS CAN BE READ AS STAND-ALONE READS WITHIN THESE SERIES

ABOUT THE AUTHOR

Alexis Winter is a contemporary romance author who loves to share her steamy stories with the world. She specializes in billionaires, alpha males and the women they love.

If you love to curl up with a good romance book you will certainly enjoy her work. Whether it's a story about an innocent young woman learning about the world or a sassy and fierce heroin who knows what she wants you,'re sure to enjoy the happily ever afters she provides.

When Alexis isn't writing away furiously, you can find her exploring the Rocky Mountains, traveling, enjoying a glass of wine or petting a cat.

You can find her books on Amazon or here:
https://www.alexiswinterauthor.com/

Made in the USA
Monee, IL
30 September 2021